Echo of the Past

Forgotten Worlds, Volume 2

Prudence MacLeod

Published by Prudence MacLeod, 2023.

Echo of the Past
(Second edition)
by
Prudence MacLeod
Copyright 5/23/2018

ECHO OF THE PAST

First edition. November 3, 2023.

Copyright © 2023 Prudence MacLeod.

ISBN: 978-1927478202

Written by Prudence MacLeod.

Chapter #1

Final Entry

Struggling to draw breath, Morthel forced down the well of sorrow and fear. Gently patting the cold dead form of her lover, she fought to draw breath and continue her diary entry. "Antha has gone now, she has not drawn a breath for some time, and she grows cold. I'm the last survivor.

"It's only been a day since something hit the planet, stripping away much of the atmosphere, and pushing us out in the system to a deeper orbit. The power has failed, and the cold of space is creeping in.

"The collision destroyed two thirds of the fleet, so only a chosen few could leave the planet. Even though thousands were killed by the quakes some people still had to remain behind. I lost the draw of lots, and sweet Antha wouldn't go without me. She stayed with me and so we will lie here, side by side for all eternity.

"I hope someone will find this diary one day and know by it all the joys of the colony, and of its sudden and unexpected demise." She pulled her dead lover closer as the racking cough from breathing the frozen atmosphere took her life, the diary still gripped tightly in a hand that no longer trembled from the cold.

Time passed, and the broken colony lay quiet on the surface of a planet that could no longer sustain life. Ages rolled by while the small shelters gazed toward the sparkling stars, the feeble light of the now distant sun no longer able to warm the planet. Eventually, even the beacons failed and stopped sending out their pleas for help, dust settled, and bodies disappeared beneath it.

Eons passed before the silent shelters felt another footstep, but these were larger feet of a different species, and even if the machines had power, the strange new voices would not have been able to activate them.

* * * * *

The small ship, Explorer settled to the frozen ground and spilled out her crew. They began to search through the ruins, eventually arriving at the resting place of Morthel and Antha.

"Carefully, now, Mr. Sacumbtu, carefully. We want to keep anything we find fully intact."

"Understood, Commander Drake. I've about got the doorway cleared now. I'll use a vac blower to suck out the dust and blow it away, so we can see what's inside."

Great clouds of dust rose into the cold thin air and drifted away as he worked. The same for three others who worked at different shelter domes nearby. Eventually he turned off the machine and called out to his leader. "Commander Drake, I think we're ready here. Do you want to go in first?"

"You know I do," she replied, excitement clear in her voice.

Light penetrated the small habitat for the first time in eons, casting eerie shadows as the tall explorer entered and cast the beam around the first room. As she entered a smaller room she found Morthel with Antha held in her arms, still embracing, frozen in that pose of eternal love and death.

"Holy smokes! People, I've got mummies here. Do we have any way to protect and transport them back to the Reacher?"

"Lilly here, Commander. We can use one of my sample crates. There's nothing alive here for me to take home."

"Thanks, Lilly. Bring a crate and a couple of guys to carry it. We'll have to be ultra-careful; I have no idea how brittle these guys might be. We'll have to keep them cold too."

Another woman soon arrived with two men carrying a large crate. The two mummified bodies were gently loaded inside, she set the environmental controls, then the men took the crate and stored it aboard Explorer One. While this was being done the commander checked in with the rest of the crew.

"Report, people, how are we doing?"

"Thirteen here, Commander. We've found lots of tech, probably junk, but we're salvaging it anyway."

"Three here, Commander Drake. I've got something on sensors about a kilometer away. It almost looks like a ship. Should we check that out?"

"Indeed we should. Take Hal and Thirteen with you, Three."

"On our way."

Commander Amanda Drake watched as her ship rose into the air and slowly moved away. When it stopped, she could still see it, but only just. She still marveled that the SUVI, super powered former slaves all, still retained their slave numbers as names by their own choice. The air supply of her enviro suit was running low before her ship returned. She ordered everyone back inside then sealed it up tight.

With a sigh of relief Amanda removed her helmet. "Ah, fresh air at last. Three, take us up to a stable orbit then everybody relax; we'll grab a meal then see where we are from there."

They gathered in the seating area of the small ship and enjoyed a meal of warm rations. "I wonder what's really in this stuff," mused one of the maintenance men.

"You don't want to know," chuckled another.

Amanda smiled as she listened. They'd endured two weeks crammed inside the small ship only to arrive at a cold frozen planet. A planet that had suffered a catastrophic event far in the past, by the size of that crater on the far side of the world.

This side had held a few surprises though, intact habitats, lots of alien tech, and several damaged ships. The settling dust from the main event had covered and protected the ships nicely. She sighed as she finished her meal and began the conversation. "Hal, Thirteen, report. What's the story on the alien ship?"

Hal White, security man on this mission shook his head and replied. "For the most part, it appears to be mainly intact, but it obviously took a major hit and wouldn't fly, otherwise they'd have used it to escape the planet."

"Thirteen, your thoughts?"

The SUVI held no rank by their own choice, but Thirteen was Amanda's self-appointed bodyguard as well as her teacher. "I think it'll be a bugger to get off the ground."

"What??? No, don't say it. Hal, if he tells me to use my brain, shoot him." Both men chuckled at that. "All right, we came looking for alien tech, there's a shipload of it right there, we can't explore it or its potential while wearing enviro suits, so the answer is to take it with us and explore it in the Reacher's cargo bay. Ensign Whang, you're the chief engineer, how do we get that ship home to the Reacher?"

"The short answer is, we tow it. The hard part will be to get it into space."

"Will our transporter shift it out?"

"No, it's half buried under rock. We'd burn out the transporter trying to shift that much mass, but if we can get it loose we can grapple it to the Explorer and take it home that way."

Amanda thought for a moment. "What about the rock holding it down, can we move that with the transporter?"

"No, same problem."

Amanda sighed and looked thoughtful, then she saw the grin on Hal's face. "Okay, Hal, what did I miss?"

"We have a couple of laser drills with us, maybe the boys would like to play."

"How about it, Mr. Sacumbtu, you guys think you can cut away the rock?"

"I haven't seen it," he replied, "but I can't imagine why we couldn't."

"All right, we have a plan. Lilly, have you tucked in our passengers?"

Lilly Peters, the ship's botanist, sighed. "The lovers are in cold storage, Commander."

"You look disappointed, Lilly."

"I'm a botanist, and this is a dead planet, nothing for me to do. My crates are full of mummies and alien tech instead of unique and interesting plants. I'll admit it, I'm a little bummed out."

"Relax girl, once we get back to the Reacher we'll be on our way to a whole new planet, and I'm told it's right where it's supposed to be. You'll have lots to do, don't worry."

There was a round of chuckles at that, then SUVI 3, ship's pilot, put the ship in a standard orbit and everyone retired to the sleeping quarters.

Pale sunlight had barely reached the damaged ship when the explorers returned. An hour later the laser drills had removed the offending rock, the grapple lines were attached, and for the first time in millennia, the wounded ship rose from the ground. It was half a million years too late, but Morthel and Antha finally escaped the planet of doom.

Chapter #2

Waiting

The captain's job is never an easy one, and Captain Suvi-jean Sorenson was keenly aware of that when she made the decision to send Explorer One away for a long mission under the command of her lover, Commander Drake. She was missing Amanda, but she'd remained on the Reacher to head off an uprising among the passengers.

Rising from runaway slave to captain in a few short months might seem like a fairy tale come true to most, but it wasn't. Commanding a ship the size of the Reacher was a difficult job, had far too many moving parts, and many of those had become rusty through time and complacency.

It was about this time when everyone aboard the Reacher slowly began to understand why Suvi-jean Sorenson had been catapulted to the Captain's chair so quickly. She, and she alone had the complete trust of the SUVI, her SUVI mind could focus on several things at once, and she was a natural leader. Things were about to get exciting for she was planning to shake things up.

In Engineering, Chief Engineer Moira Duncan sighed and tore her gaze away from the schematic on her screen. As she rubbed the kinks from her neck she spotted one of her new assistants, working busily at the one piece of alien technology they had managed to recover. "Linsey, are you buggering with that tech again?"

"Sorry, Commander. I'll stop."

Just then the captain walked in. She was searching for a certain individual and expected to find her here. "Good afternoon, busy people, anything exciting going on?"

"Not a damn thing, Captain. We're interstellar, everybody's bored, even you."

"Moira, have you gone psychic on me?"

"Suvi-jean?"

"You said I'm bored, what makes you think that?"

"This is the third time you've been in here this week, you're missing your lady companion, and you always look hopeful when you ask about excitement."

Suvi-jean Sorenson, Captain of the Reacher, last of the human built starships, laughed at that. "That easy to read, am I?"

"Ahh, we all are, Jeannie. Take Linsey there, she can't stop fussing with that alien tech, driving me nuts, and in truth it shouldn't bother me at all."

"But we're interstellar, and after all the excitement from Elysium, you're bored and cranky too?"

"Yes, and I admit it freely," chuckled the chief engineer.

The captain turned to the small woman who was unconsciously allowing her fingers to lightly caressed the alien object. "You're Linsey da Silva, correct? Tell me, Linsey, what is it about that object that so fascinates you?"

"Captain, I'm sorry, I'll stop ..."

"Relax, woman. Just tell me what's so special about that bit of alien tech?"

"It's the language, Captain."

"The language? It's a language? You can understand it?"

"No, at least not yet. It's a puzzle that's driving me crazy." Seeing the captain's raised eyebrow, she hurriedly went on. "Languages are a hobby of mine. We have hundreds of different ones stored in audio files. I learn one, and then seek out someone on the ship who is descended from whatever ethnic group developed the language, and then help them to learn it if I can. That way we can keep them all, the languages, alive."

"And you believe the information on this device to be a language?"

"All information stored is in language, Captain, how else could anyone understand it? Why store it if it's indecipherable anyway?"

"That does makes sense. So, this alien language is a tough puzzle?"

"It's maddening, Captain. The problem is, we're not sure what it's about. Is it about astronomy, engineering, or perhaps hydroponics? Each of those has its own unique jargon, so ..."

"I see the problem. It's a puzzle of galactic proportions and you want to solve it, correct?"

"I'm sorry, Captain, I just can't seem to help myself. I'll ..."

She stopped speaking as the captain held up her hand. "What's your rank?"

"Captain? Wait, Spaceman Second Class."

"Moira, I need to steal Linsey away from you. Can you spare her?"

"She's all yours, Jeannie."

The captain turned back to the young woman and smiled. "Linsey da Silva, Spaceman Second Class, I now promote you to the rank of Ensign. You will report directly to me. Your main task will be to decipher that alien language. Understanding their language would be an incredible advantage if we find more of their tech, or if we actually stumble across some of them one day.

"Now, take this artifact with you, go see the First Officer and get an office assigned for you to work in. Tell me what else you will need."

Wide eyed the girl stared at her, then shook off the mood. "Actually, Captain, I have no real idea what I'll need. Language can be incredibly intuitive, and without a native speaker to listen to, or someone with an interest to bounce ideas off ..."

"Intuitive? All right, you'll need help. SUVI 18 is psychic, and as intuitive as they come. She can help you." She reached for her comm unit. "Captain to SUVI 18."

"Eighteen here, Captain."

"Eighteen, I've got a project for you. As soon as she gets her office set up, Ensign Linsey da Silva will contact you. You two will work on this together."

"Understood, Captain."

Smiling, the captain returned her attention to the young woman. "Ensign Linsey da Silva, why are you still here?"

That snapped her out of her inaction. With a laugh of pure delight, and clutching the alien information tablet to her, she fled Engineering. Moira Duncan sighed and grinned. "Jeannie, thanks for that. You know she hasn't a hope of figuring it out."

"Maybe, but if she can, that will be an incredibly useful tool. I'll be on the bridge, let me know if anything at all exciting happens."

"You'll be the first," chuckled Moira as she returned her attention to her schematics.

* * * * *

The captain headed for the bridge but detoured to the Chief of Security's office. She found him, Brandon Hoffman, his second in command, Sheila Singh, and, her self-appointed big brother, Jake White. "Welcome, Captain."

"Thank you, Brandon. How is that list coming?"

"You gave me forty-seven names, Jeannie. I've only managed to get evidence on thirty-two of them, but I have plenty to convict all of those."

"You look ill, Sub-Commander Singh, are you all right?"

"I'm sorry, Captain. I honestly thought I'd seen everything, but the depravity of what was happened to you and the rest of the SUVI down on that colony turns my stomach. These diaries, personal logs, what was done to you and the others, especially to that twelve year old girl, Melanie ..."

"She is SUVI 18 now, Sheila. She survived, as I did."

I know, Jeannie, I know, but ... I can't even ..."

"Jake, your thoughts?"

"Blow them out the airlock, little sister, every fucking one of them."

The captain sighed and sank into a chair. "I confess, that is my first thought and my desire, but sadly, that we cannot do. They must face a fair trial as did the others."

"So, what will we do with them once they're convicted, as they surely will be?" asked Brandon Hoffman. "Personally, I'm with Jake on this one."

"For now, they go into the brig. If convicted they will remain there until we find someplace to dump them off. We're holding the ship here for a few days until Amanda catches up. With luck we can get those trials finished before she gets back."

"So it's a go?"

"It's a go, Jake. Haul them in, interrogate them, see if you can get anything on the rest of that list. Brandon, once you've got them all locked up, take the evidence to Olga, ask her to set up the trials."

"The official charges?"

"Rape, assault, murder, aggravated assault, assault causing bodily harm, and torture, that should be a good start."

"Aye, Captain. Sheila, you and Jake all set?"

"We are boss, the men are already waiting."

"Then go make the arrests. Where will you be, Captain?"

"I'll be on the bridge." With that she rose and walked out.

* * * * *

Linsey da Silva sat in her new office staring at the alien tech lying on her shiny new desk. She was completely lost in thought, and unaware as the door opened and someone entered. A throat being cleared made Linsey shriek and leap to her feet, her hand over her heart.

A small woman was standing just inside the door, trying to hide her smile. "Sorry, didn't mean to startle you. Are you Ensign da Silva?"

"What? Oh, yes I am and no, you're not."

"Excuse me?"

"Sorry. You're not sorry, you're laughing at me."

"I'm not." Eighteen tried, but the arched eyebrow aimed at her forced the laugh past her lips.

That laugh sounded rusty, long unused, and it broke through Linsey's feigned indignation. With a bright smile, she extended her hand. "I'm Linsey, welcome to our new home."

Tentatively, SUVI 18 shook the offered hand. "I truly am sorry, Ensign da Silva. I shouldn't have laughed at you. What did you mean, our new home?"

"Don't be sorry, I'm sure it was funny, and if the situation was reversed, I'd have laughed at you. Right, new home. Eighteen, my new friend, you and I have the unenviable task of solving the greatest mystery to face humanity since the dawn of time."

"Oh? What is it?"

"The alien language." Linsey passed her the tablet. "All information stored, is stored in language, right?"

Eighteen gazed at the object in her hand. "Yes, what you say makes sense, but there's no way for us to understand this language ... that's the task you speak of, correct?"

"It is. We have to figure this out. I expect we'll spend a lot of time in this office, racking our brains. You sound out of practice."

"I expect we will. What???"

"Your laugh, I liked the sound of it, but it sounded rusty, unused."

"Very perceptive, Ensign. I haven't had a lot to laugh about."

Linsey reached out to lightly grip her arm. "Eighteen, I'm sorry for that. I can't even imagine what you must have endured on Elysium. We need a code word."

SUVI 18 smiled and chuckled softly. "Ensign da Silva, are you sure you're not SUVI?"

"Linsey, remember? What do you mean?"

"Your mind, it easily focuses on several things at once. That's a strong SUVI trait, it just surprised me in a human. The code word?"

"Everybody says I'm a scatterbrain. Right, code word. We need a word to tell me when I need to shut up and mind my own business. Eighteen, I don't want to offend you, pry into your past, or remind you of things you'd rather forget. When you speak the magic word, I'll know to shut up and change the subject."

"Linsey, I know you didn't mean to offend me. Twenty."

"Thanks for that. Twenty? Oh, the code word. Okay, but why that one?"

"There are nineteen SUVI, but as I said, you have the mind of a SUVI, so ..."

Linsey laughed with delight. "Twenty it is."

"Music."

"Of course, why didn't I think of that. We could try assigning a musical tone to each of these symbols, see what that does for us." She smiled brightly at her new friend, but SUVI 18 was almost in a trance. "Eighteen?"

Shaking off the vision, SUVI 18 turned to Linsey. "We can play with it for a while, but there's no hurry right now."

"Talk to me, woman."

"Explorer should be back any day now, and I just had the strongest sense they will be bringing treasures for us to explore."

For three days they looked at the screens, tried audio hook-ups, and more, discussed ideas at length, and built the basics of a friendship. SUVI 18 was guarded, but Linsey's bubbly personality had her laughing more and more.

For her part, Linsey sensed the depths of this poor wounded soul's anguish. Slavery must have been a special hell for this gentle intuitive woman. Linsey silently vowed to make her laugh at least once every day.

SUVI 18 knew, of course, and was both bemused and amazed that this woman, a full human, would do this for her, a former slave.

* * * * *

On the planet of Elysium, an attempted human colony failed, the survivors had tried to capture the Reacher and escape their fate. They failed in that attempt, but were taken aboard the Reacher as refugees anyway. Much to the horror of many of these refugees, one of their former slaves, SUVI 5, became the captain, leaving them unsure and concerned about what fate now held in store for them.

While Linsey and Eighteen sat puzzling over the ultimate enigma, a troupe of security people swept through the ship, thirty-two people were arrested and tossed in the brig. By the next morning several more had joined them as the prisoners gave evidence against their fellows. A few hours later the Captain sat in her private quarters, facing an angry man, the former captain of the Reacher, her grandfather.

"Is it true, Jeannie? Did you have dozens of colonists arrested?"

"Yes, it's true. Do I detect a note of censure in your voice, Grandfather?"

"Why? Why were they arrested en masse?"

"They were arrested, and will face charges, for assault, rape, murder, and more. I wanted at least forty-seven of them brought to justice, but Brandon could only find evidence against thirty-two. Those gave him evidence against more. They all will face trial tomorrow. Olga is now reviewing the evidence against them. Should they be found guilty they will face the repercussions of their actions."

"We agreed that we were going to leave all that behind, to save as many humans as possible ..."

"No, you decided that, you and you alone, even though you were aware of what these people had done. However, that was easy for you, you've never worn a pain collar, you've never been strapped down and had your body invaded while the collar was turned up to make you scream."

Frank Baris could not meet her eyes. "What of their right to a fair trial? Will they be defended?"

"Defended? Who was there to defend Melanie Merkel? You might know her as SUVI 18. She was twelve years old, still sick, when she was fitted with the collar then held down and raped by five men while the collar was turned on. The rest of the other SUVI were forced to stand and watch.

"The man who organized that incident is dead, but the men who took part are now in the brig. They will face trial for those and many other such actions, whippings, beatings, and the like."

Her eyes were glowing amber now and he sat very quietly in his chair while she paced like a tigress. He had seen her at full SUVI the day she came aboard the ship. Frank Baris knew only too well what his granddaughter was capable of, and it frightened him. "You brought those people aboard, refused to hold them accountable, then retired and left me to deal with the mess. So, this is me, a SUVI, dealing with the fallout.

"If it eases your mind any, this was done at the request of Gordo Irda, a grounder himself, but a man who objected to the enslavement of the SUVI. Farouk Bladon allowed him to live because he needed the man's medical skills. The investigation was conducted by Brandon and Sheila Singh. Those men will face Olga Volkov in trial, all people involved are full human, no SUVI has taken part in this except me."

"You?"

"I gave Brandon a list of people to investigate, nothing more."

"Jeannie ..."

"Grandfather, I'm SUVI, not human, your moral codes have no meaning for me, nor do your laws as such. By your own choice I am now the leader here, it's now my task to protect the people, both SUVI and human. This is not an exercise in revenge, this is a culling of the herd. The pedophiles, rapists, the excessively violent, and the murders will be removed for the greater good.

"I wanted to do this in the beginning, but you wouldn't hear of it. You brought them up here where they can endanger the ship and the people on her. You refused to let me deal with them quickly, and as a result the virus that made the SUVI what we are was nearly let loose on the ship.

"Now they're here, and a man who abused Amanda as a child, and me as an adult, was caught trying to take another child. The child's father lodged the complaint that set this in motion."

"What are you going to do with them?"

Something in his voice caught her attention. She looked closely at him and saw the distress there. "Grandfather, I'm not angry with you, I'm just frustrated. Worse, I've become dependent on Mandy's cool head to keep me grounded, and she's not here to help me.

"I confess I'm struggling a bit to keep my actions within human parameters. My SUVI self wants to transport them out into free space, be rid of the danger to the many, and rid us of the drain on resources.

"What I plan to do with them? They'll be housed in the brig until I can find a planet to leave them on. If you have a better idea, I'm wide open to suggestions."

Frank Baris sighed and melted deeper in to the chair. He suddenly realized the magnitude of the mistake his adherence to his own personal codes and been. He had truly hamstrung the people trying to help him, then dumped the lot in his granddaughter's lap. It was time to suck it up and make amends.

"Well, you could get Eamon to put them into cryo sleep. You could hold them in stasis until you find a likely planet, then isolate them on a continent far away from the rest of the population."

Suvi-jean nodded, looking thoughtful. "I like it. I'll offer it up to Olga as a possibility."

"Jeannie, I realize now I dumped a heavy load on you, and you're right, I have no experience of a slave's life. However, I do know just how hard your job is, and I have to admit you're adjusting to it a lot faster than I did at your age."

"But you have concerns."

"I know you use that genetic memory of yours to access my past for a guideline, but I'm getting the sense you're using another guide as well."

"He was a Viking raider, a truly violent man in a violent time, but he was successful, his people loved him, and willingly followed him. Between you I'm trying to find a path, a style of leadership that will help me in this day and age."

He chuckled at that. "So how's that going for you?"

She sighed and sank into her chair. "It's a work in progress."

Chapter #3

Treasure

"Battle stations, battle stations, Captain to the bridge."

That call sent Suvi-jean flying from her bed. She came pounding onto the bridge. "Commander Jones, report."

Emmet Jones, second Officer on the Reacher, and the man in charge of all things on the bridge, turned to her. "Captain, we've made contact with an unknown object. We hailed it, and it responded that it was the Explorer. Captain, whatever that thing is, it's far too large to be Explorer One."

"They're hailing us again." That voice came from the communications station.

"Put them up on screen."

"Aye Captain."

Amanda Drake's face appeared on the big screen. "Reacher, this is Explorer One, please respond."

SUVI-jean stepped closer. "Unknown object, this is Captain Sorenson of the Reacher. Identify yourself properly and explain why you have taken our people prisoner."

"Prisoner? Oh crap. Jeannie, your instruments are showing an object twice the size of the Explorer, aren't they?"

"Yes."

"Okay, give us an hour and it all should become clear. I strongly suggest you make some room in the cargo bay. You wanted alien tech, so we salvaged a ship for you. That's why your instruments are showing us so big, we're towing a damaged ship. Make room and have lots of emergency people waiting. Getting this monster inside won't be easy."

"You salvaged a ship?"

"Yes we did, and we picked up a couple of passengers too."

"Amanda, are you teasing me?"

Her laughter brought a smile to the captain's face. "I am, Captain. We found two mummies, locked in an embrace. Lilly calls them the lovers. Carla wants to alert Dr. Reilly to have cold storage ready. We're coming home loaded."

"I'll be waiting at the cargo bay. Reacher out. Stand down battle stations, Mr. Jones."

"Aye, Captain. Captain, I ..."

"You did right, Emmet. You had an unknown object on instruments that was making noises like it belonged to us yet didn't look like it. Err on the side of caution, that's the official policy. Now, I leave the bridge to you, I'm going down to see what the heck is going on." He chuckled to himself as she walked away.

Suvi-jean reached the cargo bay where she joined SUVI 18 and Linsey who were waiting with the chief engineer. Together they watched as the big doors began to slide back. Once they were open she could see the wreck of the alien ship floating freely with the Explorer nearby. Slowly Explorer began to nudge the wreck toward the open doors.

The ship banged against the side of the Reacher, then bounced back into the Explorer. After two more failed attempts, Explorer One opened up and three people in space suits floated out to take hold of the derelict ship. The explorer eased closer so they could plant their feet to push, then they guided the ship inside. Once through they released the cables and withdrew to their own ship.

The small ship pulled back, the doors closed, then gravity was returned to the cargo bay. People on machines appeared, locked onto the wreck, and moved it out of the way. Once there was room, they withdrew, the doors opened, and Explorer One swept in and landed.

As it lightly touched down SUVI 18 spoke. "They have dead people aboard that ship. Long, long dead, but I can feel them."

"Are you enjoying your new job, Eighteen?"

"I am, Five. Linsey is a delight to work for."

"With, Eighteen," said Linsey. "We're in this together, remember?"

"Yes Linsey, together. Perhaps there will be more information for us to work with now."

"It's those dead people that interest me."

That caught the captain's attention. "Why those, Linsey?"

"I hope they found some things near them, personal things. Info caches like a diary or something that held no technical jargon would make our task a lot easier."

"Then I give you full authorization to access or take control of anything they brought back. Linsey, up to now your task was a fun exercise, now it has just become vital. We need to understand these people and to be able to communicate with them, if at all possible. At the least, knowing how to read their language will give us a wealth of information.

"Take charge of whatever you want, and we'll meet tomorrow for a briefing." With that the captain stepped away to catch the commander of Explorer One in an embrace.

Tentatively Linsey approached the buzz of activity around the salvaged ship and Explorer One. The chief engineer was directing the organized chaos as they approached. "Linsey, this isn't a good time to come poking around."

"Sorry, Commander Duncan, but the captain gave me the authority to take control of any and all salvage or stored information recovered by Explorer One."

"She did what? We'll just see about that. Engineering to the Captain."

"Sorenson here. What's up, Moira?"

"I've got Ensign da Silva here claiming you gave her my job."

There was laughter in the Captain's voice as she replied. "Give her whatever she needs, Moira. Our future, and ultimate fate may well lie in her ability to succeed."

Linsey took a step back and cringed as the chief engineer sighed and turned to her. "All yours, Ensign da Silva."

"Commander, I don't want to mess with you, I don't. Right now all I want is information about the two bodies they brought in. Was there any stored information found near them?"

"No idea, let's ask Lilly Peters." Moira Duncan waved her arm and caught the attention of a young woman supervising several men. She approached. "Ensign Peters, this is Ensign da Silva. The captain's given her control of all the salvage."

"Ensign da Silva, what do you need?"

"First, I'm not interested in control of the salvage, I've just been given access to any and all of the stored information. You brought two bodies back. Was there any stored information found near them?"

"One of them was holding a tablet of some sort; Carla said it could be a diary or a journal. You know, recording their last moments."

"Oh my, that would be perfect! Where is it?"

"Still in the mummy's hand as far as I know. Carla took the crate with the bodies to the infirmary lab. Apparently, Dr. Reilly is all excited."

"So am I. See you later." With that she was off at a run, leaving the chief engineer scratching her head.

Linsey hurried into the infirmary with SUVI 18 close behind her. She was headed toward the lab at the back when the chief medical officer stepped in her path. "Whoa there, what's the emergency?"

"Two alien bodies were brought in here. I need to get to them."

"Hold on, hold on, you're not authorized to ..."

"Yes I am. The captain gave me access to anything and everything from the salvage. I'm told one ..."

"Just a minute here. Healing bay to the captain."

"Captain here. What's up, Eamon?"

"Jeannie, there's a young woman here who ..."

"Ensign da Silva?"

The doctor peered at the girl's name tag. "Yes, that ..."

"Give her whatever she wants."

"But Captain ..."

"All right, let's deal with this right now." Suddenly the captain's voice came over ship's speakers. "This is the captain, all senior staff to the bridge. Ensign Linsey da Silva, SUVI 18, to the bridge."

They all swiftly gathered at the bridge briefing room. Linsey gulped and sat staring at her hands while the captain paced, her eyes glowing amber. "Are we all here?"

"All present and accounted for, Captain," grinned the First Officer.

"Thank you, Commander Volkov. Very well then. People, Explorer One has brought us a wealth of possibilities, as well as a reminder and a warning. We are not alone. Somewhere out there in the endless reaches of space, is another species with interstellar capabilities, at least one, perhaps many more. At the present we know of only one, and that one preceded us by millennia.

"Now, we have several problems. We managed to decipher a star chart they left behind, a chart that allows us to back track their progress. Explorer has returned with a damaged ship, more information, and examples of their physiology. The main issue facing us at this point is language, or lack of it.

"People, we need to decipher that alien language. If we can do that we can then read their manuals, specs, charts, etc. Plus, should we ever encounter them in the flesh, we will be able to communicate with them.

"Things we need to know: are they friendly, are they a race of explorers or are they conquerors, a race of peaceful people or a warrior society?

"This has been on my mind as of late, and I've spent considerable time poring over personnel records to find someone to solve this puzzle for us. There is only one person that stood out, and I found her trying to solve that very puzzle in engineering.

"Ensign da Silva, I now promote you to the rank of sub-commander. You know your task, and the rest of us will do all in our power to make that possible for you to accomplish. Tell us what you need."

Stunned, Linsey sat staring at the captain, her mouth working, but no sound coming out. SUVI 18 nudge her gently and whispered. "The diary."

"What, oh, yes, forgive me Captain, and thank you for the promotion. Yes, what I need. There were two alien bodies brought in by Explorer. I'm told one of them was holding an information tablet of some kind. That will probably be a diary or personal journal or something like that. It will be written without technical jargon and will be my best bet ..."

"Now hold on," said Dr. Reilly. "Look, first that mummy is holding that thing tightly, I'd have to thaw both of them out to get it loose. Why can't you use something else?"

The captain nodded to Linsey, who nervously rose to her feet. "Doctor, if you put a medical journal on this table I could read it. I couldn't understand it, but I could read it because I already have the language it was written in.

"If the chief engineer put an advanced schematic discussion paper on the table I could read it, but not understand it even though my training is in engineering. Too advanced, but I have the language to read it.

"However, if I put my own diary on the table you could all read and understand it."

"You sure about that?" chuckled Moira Duncan. "All right, Linsey, we get it. The diary, and or any personal logs from the ship, are what you need at first. We need to learn the language before we can hope to understand the rest."

"Now wait ..." The doctor gulped as the captain turned and faced him directly, her eyes glowing amber. Eamon Reilly had never seen her at full SUVI, and it frightened him.

"Explain your objections."

"Well, I ... Dammit, Jeannie, they were obviously lovers, locked in the final embrace, together for all time. If we just break off the fingers to get the tablet, then we're nothing more than grave robbers. It's disrespectful of the dead and their entire race. This is something our ancestors would do, but I'll have no part of it."

The captain sighed and forcibly relaxed her shoulders. "Hear me well, people. By your own choice I am captain here. I've sworn to act in the best interests of all, the survival of the last of humanity, for the greater good. If there's anyone in this room who can't set aside their personal codes and comforts for the greater good, then take off your insignia and leave. I'll appoint another to your station."

No one spoke a word but sat in stunned silence. Finally the commander of Explorer One broke the spell. "Easy, Captain. Let me." Amanda Drake patted the captain's arm as she rose to stand beside her.

"By all means, Mandy, find us a way out of this impasse." The captain resumed her pacing.

Amanda relaxed back into her seat then smiled at Linsey. "Sub-commander da Silva, would not one of the personal logs from the ship serve your purpose just as well?"

"Of course it would, Commander. The problem is, how do I tell a personal log from a technical manual? There's no way to know without understanding the language. That tablet gripped in the cadaver's hand is by far the best bet, unless I've missed something. I'm wide open to suggestions here."

Eamon Reilly sighed and slumped back in his chair. "She's right. I apologize, Sub-Commander da Silva, you're absolutely right, that damn tablet is your best bet for a starting point. I sure as hell don't envy you the task before you, but I'll get you the tablet, that is, if I still have a job."

The captain's eyes slowly returned to green as she sank into her chair. "You still have a job if you want it."

"Jeannie, I ..."

"That's the second time you've blocked me, Eamon. First you insisted on keeping that virus on the ship even though I wanted to transport it out into space."

"Jeannie, it's perfectly safe in the lab."

"No, it isn't, and you know it. It's there and a threat to the all people on this ship, but I trust you to keep us safe from it. That time your natural leanings as a researcher balked me and I allowed it.

"This time your personal code of ethics blocked progress on a vital mission. This can't happen again, ever."

"Jeannie ..."

"No. My grandfather ignored my instincts and allowed the invasion of the ship, placing everyone in danger, many were injured, and some were killed. He then allowed his personal code of ethics to override me again and he brought the grounders up to the ship, every damned one of them.

"He then forgave them of every crime they had committed against me and the rest of the SUVI. We went through hell as slaves, and now we're forced to face those people every day, we're expected to forgive and forget like it never happened.

"Grandfather then retired and left me with the mess his dogmatic adherence to those codes had created. On top of that, I have a deadly virus on this ship in the care of a man who doesn't trust my judgement and feels quite free to gainsay me whenever the mood takes him. Never again, Eamon.

"Sub-commander da Silva is now officially the interspecies communications officer of this ship, and as such will be part of all senior staff meetings. She is to have full and instant access to anything and everything alien.

"People, I can hear objections, and I can listen to advice, you all know this. However, your personal codes, your personal opinions and desires, must always take second place to the greater good. Come to me with logic, sounds reasons, hell, even a strong hunch, and I'll hear you, we'll work it out together for the greater good."

The captain leaned her elbows on the table, her eyes beginning to glow amber again. "Eamon, this next thing will be difficult for you, and if you wish, I'll put Carla in charge of it."

"Captain?"

"Linsey needs that tablet, and I want those people thawed out, thawed out and rehydrated, studied, examined, and more. I want to know what they looked like, how alike are our physiologies are, how similar an environment can we inhabit, and more. We need to learn everything we can about these people as quickly as possible.

"Perhaps there are more or partial cadavers on the ship you can examine for much of this information, but I still want them thawed out and re-hydrated." The doctor began to visibly tremble.

"All right, people, is there any further business?" No one spoke. "Very well then, meeting adjourned. Dr. Reilly, Commander Drake, and Commander Volkov, a word in private, please." The others filed out and shut the door.

The captain turned back to the doctor. "Eamon, what is it? What is it about these people that has you so distraught?"

"Better tell her, Eamon," said Olga Volkov, First Officer of the Reacher.

"All right, Olga, I'll confess my sins. Better yet, you do it while I get hold of my emotions."

"All right, old friend, sit back and collect yourself. Jeannie, the good doctor has a wife, she got deathly ill thirty years ago, and he put her in cryo-sleep until he could find a cure. She's on this ship. Tara's frozen, like our two new passengers. The thought of thawing them out has messed him up a bit."

"You knew this all along and didn't tell me?"

"I didn't tell anyone. Eamon Reilly is the best doctor alive, and I fought to get him assigned to my ship, and again to bring him aboard the Reacher when we blended the crews."

"Did Grandfather know?"

"No, nor did Brandon, I helped Eamon smuggle her aboard. There's not a lot to do when we're interstellar, so he had plenty of time for his research."

The captain nodded then turned to the Doctor. "That's why you were so excited about the berries I brought aboard, and why you wanted to keep the virus. You hoped the virus could defeat her physical disease and the berries could restore her mind."

"Yes. It was the first time in years I've had any hope at all."

"Of all the ..."

"Jeannie sweetie ..."

"I know, Mandy, I know, for the greater good." The captain sighed and squeezed her lover's hand. "Eamon, thaw them out, rehydrate them, revive them if you can, and if not learn what you can from them before we give them a burial in Space with full honors. Above all, get that damned diary into Linsey's hands as quickly as possible.

"Once you're done with the aliens, hand the ship's medical staff over to Carla and focus all your efforts on the project of your wife."

"What??? Jeannie, are you serious?"

"I am, Eamon. You will be the Chief of Medical Research. Get Linsey to work then focus on bringing back your lover. And for god's sake, be careful with that damned virus."

"Jeannie, I don't know what to say. I ..."

"Go on, get out of here and get to work." With a look of relief and anticipation, he fled the briefing room.

"So, am I going to lose my job too?"

"Not a chance, Olga, you're not that lucky. Now, are there any more deep dark secrets aboard this ship I should know about?"

"Nope, that's it as far as I'm aware. We kept it secret because Captain Baris would've had a fit, demoted Eamon, and forbidden him access to the lab."

"Yes, well, I'm not my grandfather. As you say, Eamon's the best, and we need the best. We need him at his best. Once he has his lover back I want him to teach Carla everything he can."

"Captain, you amaze me once again. As angry as you were with him, you helped him, granted his deepest desire, then let him go."

"Demoting and punishing him would avail me nothing and be a harm to the population. My personal feelings are irrelevant, my job is to serve the greater good." Once again First Officer Volkov was amazed at the way a SUVI's mind worked. She smiled to herself as she walked away, they'd made the right choice for captain.

Chapter #4

The Lovers Revealed

Eamon Reilly arrived back at the infirmary to find Ensign Marks facing down an excited Linsey da Silva. "I'm sorry, Sub-Commander, but without Dr. Reilly's consent I can't ..."

"Give her whatever she wants, Carla. The captain gave her complete control of all the salvage, all things alien. The captain also wants us to thaw the lovers out and rehydrate them."

"Rehydrate them? Seriously? Wow. All right, I'll get the process started. How soon do you want that tablet, Sub-Commander?"

"Linsey, call me Linsey. As soon as you can get it for me without damaging the girls. Look, I don't want to control anything, the captain just did that so I could get instant access to what I might need."

"Need? For what?"

"Linsey's been tasked with learning to understand their language."

Carla turned wide eyes on Linsey. "Speak their language? Can you even do that?"

"Fingers crossed," replied Linsey, holding up her hands with crossed fingers.

"Wow. Okay, the very instant I can work that tablet free, it'll be in your hands."

"Awesome. This is so exciting; I can hardly wait. Can I see them?"

"The lovers? Sure. Right this way." Carla led them down a short corridor. "There's not much to see right now. We transferred them from Lilly's sample crate into a controlled environment capsule. In here."

They stepped into a large room where they could look down through the glass at the two freeze dried creatures still locked in a loving embrace. "Wow. Look, Eighteen, there's our tablet. Man, she sure has a grip on it. I can see the problem; you'd have to cut off all her fingers to get it out."

"They were more than lovers." Both Linsey and Carla turned to SUVI 18. She was slightly out of focus and had tears in her eyes. "I can feel them. Theirs was a forbidden love. They fled to that distant outpost, seeking safety, only to be killed by a rogue asteroid. I can feel their love for each other, the fear and eventual acceptance of impending death."

Linsey gently took SUVI 18 by the hand. "Come on girl, we need to get back to the office and get to work. Carla's got this." Without another word she led Eighteen away.

SUVI 18 had learned early to loathe and fear the touch of a human hand, but for some odd reason, the gentle grip on her fingers was comforting and she didn't pull away but allowed herself to be guided along.

As they entered the office, Linsey closed the door and turned to SUVI 18. "Okay, we're clear. Are you okay?"

"Yes. I've regained control of my emotions. Thank you for what you did for me. No one has ever shown concern for me like that before." Startled, Linsey arched an eyebrow at her. "Linsey, until this moment, every human touch has brought pain, pain and humiliation. I felt your concern for me and allowed the touch. It comforted me, in an odd way. To be touched gently, comforted, by a full human, it ..."

SUVI 18 got no further as she was suddenly enfolded in gentle arms. She froze, standing stiffly as Linsey held her. "Eighteen, relax against me, I won't hurt you, I promise." Unsure, tentative, yet driven by a need she could not name, SUVI 18 slowly relaxed into Linsey's arms.

Suddenly the dam burst, a flood of emotion overwhelmed her, and she began to sob into Linsey's shoulder. When that storm passed Linsey was leaning against the wall with a limp SUVI 18 in her arms. She cooed soothing sounds and lightly kissed the woman's hair.

The tears started again, and strong arms tightened around Linsey, giving her a glimpse into the physical strength of a SUVI. She smiled and tightened her grip as well. Slowly the tears stopped and SUVI 18 relaxed her grip. Linsey gently kissed her hair then released the hug, allowing Eighteen to step away.

"Linsey, what did you do to me?"

"I didn't do anything to you, honey, but I did do some things for you, some things that should have been done long ago. I saw you become overwhelmed by residual emotions from the cadavers. I brought you out of the public place, and once we were alone I held you while you processed those emotions."

"I can't begin to tell you how special that was for me. Linsey, you're a full human and I'm SUVI, why would you do that?"

"Because you're my friend, you're special to me, you were in pain and needed to be comforted, held, and hugged. Friends do that for each other. You'd do the same for me."

"No, I wouldn't. I might want to, but I wouldn't know how, nor would I dare to touch a full human unless ..."

Linsey reached out to grasp her hands. "Hey now, we're friends, and you can touch me anytime you want to, or feel the need. Eighteen, that talent of yours is incredible, but I bet it can be hard to live with sometimes. So, here's the deal, we're friends, you can touch me whenever you want to, and if you want or need to be touched, held, and comforted, just tell me. Say, Linsey I need a hug, and I'll hug you. Deal?"

SUVI 18 gazed at her with big soft eyes. "Deal. Linsey, you can have a hug whenever you want one too. It feels so strange, but it doesn't hurt, and it makes me feel good. Is this what being friends is like?"

"Yes it is, honey. Feeling better now?"

"I feel different somehow, but yes, I'm in control again."

Linsey thought that sounded like there was a lot more going on but didn't comment on it. "Great. Now for the next step."

"Next step?"

"Yes, after a good cry and a hug from a friend, it's traditional to go eat something. Usually we bypass the meal and go right to the desserts."

"Seriously? Is that healthy?"

"Oh heck no, but it is traditional. Come on, Eighteen, live a little." She took Eighteen by the hand and led her to the mess for a dessert binge.

* * * * *

While Eighteen and Linsey sat destroying several desserts, Dr. Carla Marks found herself getting an unexpected promotion. "Dr. Reilly are you serious?"

"Captain's orders."

"When did this happen? I mean, she's never spoken a word to me about this. I ..."

"Suvi-jean's probably just thought of it."

"I did," said the Captain as she and Commander Drake entered the infirmary. "Carla, Eamon has another project or two that will take all his time. He'll be focusing on research for the foreseeable future."

"But, Jeannie, there are lots of more senior medical people who should have the job before me."

"I did some research of my own and learned that the good doctor gave you the task of organizing the medical bay before the grounder invasion. Obviously, he felt you were the best person for the task; therefore, you get the job.

"Carla, we're far too small a population to operate on the seniority system. That system kept Jake in Sanitation when he clearly belonged in security. We'll operate on the merit system. With us, you earn your place with proven ability, not seniority.

"Under the merit system, you've proven yourself and have earned the position. Eamon will mentor you and teach you what he can. Now, do you feel you can thaw out the lovers for me, I have another task for Eamon."

"Yes, I can handle that, Jeannie."

"Then I promote you to the rank of Commander. Eamon will call the medical staff together and announce your new position as Chief of Staff.

"Now, Eamon, you have more knowledge of cryogenics than anyone. Here's what I need. There are thirty-two or more men in the brig who have been tried and sentenced to exile as soon as possible. They're a drain on resources and I want you to put them to sleep until we can find a place to safely leave them."

"My god, are you serious?"

"I am."

"All right, Jeannie, but they have to be willing to undergo the treatment."

"They will be, it's that or a quick trip outside the ship into free space. You're now in charge of all medical research. Tell Carla what you need, and she can make it happen for you. You can coordinate with the Chief of Security about how and when to put the prisoners to sleep.

"Now, Commander Marks, show me the lovers."

"Yes, Captain, right this way. I've already brought up the temperature to our norm. I have no idea if that works for them or not, but it's a start. Once they begin to thaw I'll get fluids into them, but again, I have no idea at all if they'll be the right fluids. Jeannie, honestly, there's not a chance in a million of reviving one of them."

"I know. Were there any other cadavers found in the ship?"

"Seven partials and three completes."

"Learn what you can from the partials to help you with the lovers."

"Already working on it, Captain."

"Then I leave you to it, Chief of Staff."

* * * * *

Suvi-jean returned from the bathroom to find Amanda already in the bed and waiting. "Come here, my precious girl, my fierce SUVI, come let me hold you."

Jeannie willingly snuggled into those waiting arms and hugged Amanda tightly. "I have missed this so much."

"Me too, sweetie, me too. So, is this all you missed?"

"No, I've missed the kissing thing too. It's been so long you'll have to teach me how to do it all over again."

With a sexy purr Amanda pulled her closer. "Then let the lessons begin."

Chapter #5

A Voice From the Past

The captain's table at the mess was nearly full as the new Chief of Medical Staff and her companion approached. "Sub-Commander da Silva."

Linsey looked up from her plate with a raised eyebrow. "Commander?"

"Brought you a present."

"What? Oh my god, you've got it?" Carla grinned as she pulled her hands from behind her back and passed the treasured diary to Linsey who squealed with delight. "Yes! Oh yes, that's it."

SUVI 18 didn't look nearly as happy as Linsey and Linsey noticed it. She caught Eighteen by the hand and tugged her to her feet. "Come on, Eighteen, let's get this back to the office. We've got work to do."

They arrived back at the office in record time. Eighteen stood back and watched as Linsey hooked up the tablet to the instruments and began probing for a power button. She squealed with delight as the screen lit up displaying row upon row of symbols. Slowly, Eighteen pushed back the fear and sorrow that battered at her from the diary and began to smile. Linsey's joy and enthusiasm were infectious. With a smile of her own, Eighteen joined Linsey at the monitor.

* * * * *

While the two linguists pored over the diary, an explosion in the cargo bay sent security and the captain racing to the scene of the accident. Medical was already there and working. Several people were being transported directly to the infirmary. "What happen here?"

"There was an explosion, Captain," replied one engineer. "Root cause is unknown, but it originated in the salvaged ship."

"Originated?"

"Yes Ma'am. My guess is someone triggered some sort of weapons' system. Fortunately, the hull wasn't breached."

"Injuries?"

"Nine people injured as far as I know, none fatal."

"All work on alien technology or artifacts is to cease immediately until further notice. Security, move everyone away from the salvaged ship and seal it off."

"Aye Captain."

Grumbling to herself about people who couldn't leave things alone, Suvi-jean hurried to the infirmary. Everyone was busy, and she decided to wait until later for a report. She left and went to Linsey's office.

"Captain, welcome. This is so exciting. I believe we're going to get it; we're going to figure it out."

"The sooner the better, Linsey."

"Captain?"

"There was an explosion in the cargo bay. Some fool was flipping switches to see what would happen. He triggered a weapon's system and damn near blew a hole in the Reacher's hull. I've ordered all work on that ship to stop until you give the go ahead. Once we have the language we can start reading manuals, understand warning symbols, ..."

"On it, Captain. I work as we speak."

Suvi-jean noticed the gentle smile on Eighteen's face as she watched Linsey work. Grinning to herself, the captain withdrew and returned to the infirmary.

As she entered she found Carla pulling off bloody gloves and tossing them into the garbage chute. "Carla?"

"Nine injuries, none fatal, none permanent. Five will return to work next shift, the rest within a week. Do you know what happened?"

"Someone triggered a weapon's system."

"You shut them down until Linsey can work it out?"

"Indeed I did. So, all good here?"

"Yes. Oh, Jeannie, don't go yet, I've got something to show you. Come on." She led the way to the area where the lovers were kept. The two bodies had relaxed somewhat but were still entwined. The skin was also relaxing, making them look like something from a horror story.

"They're still frozen at the core, but the exterior is softening up nicely. One of the cadavers from the ship provided me with samples of what must have been blood. We're analyzing it and hope to be able to have a cocktail close enough to re-hydrate them with. Jeannie, ..."

"I know, Carla, I know. The chances of returning one of them to life are minimal. I just want us to learn as much as we can about them. The more we know, the more we can be prepared for when we make planetfall."

"Speaking of which, the Reacher hasn't moved since Explorer returned. We're just sitting here in the middle of nowhere. Dare I ask ..."

"All right, Carla, I'll confess. I'll call a senior staff meeting this afternoon and confess all."

"Then you'll tell us later?"

"You're senior staff now, Carla. You'll be at the meeting."

"Oh, right, so I will. Jeannie, I still can't wrap my head around this."

"You're tough, you'll adjust. Has anyone given you any trouble?"

"Only one, but Dr. Reilly nearly ate him alive. I've never seen him like that before, but he burned the guy's ass good. Everybody else seems to be okay with it, that or they're sitting back waiting for me to mess it up."

"You won't mess it up, Carla."

"I'm glad you're sure."

"Girl, you took control and handled things when the grounders attacked, and again today. Don't doubt yourself, Carla. You can do this." She patted her friend on the shoulder and walked away.

"Wow, Hal was right," mused Carla as she watched the captain leave. "Don't tell Jeannie your dreams if you can't handle seeing them come true."

* * * * *

The briefing room was full as the captain entered with Commander Drake. "All right people, report."

"All quiet on the bridge, Captain."

"Thank you, Commander Jones. Security?"

"We had a minor riot in the brig, but Jake White sorted that out. A group of dissidents were marching toward the bridge, but Sub-Commander Singh headed that off. All alien tech has been locked down and is under guard."

"Thank you, Brandon, well done. Social Engagement, Commander Drake?"

"Me? Oh, yes, we've got every facility on the ship up and running, but still struggling a bit to get the grounders and sky-riders to mingle more. It's a work in progress."

The captain smiled and nodded. "Engineering?"

"I've got nothing since you shut everything down. It's boring as hell."

"Medical?"

Carla blushed as she gave her first official report. "We had a bit of excitement when someone tried to shoot his way out of the cargo bay, but no truly serious injuries. Medical research is still setting up the cryo-beds for the prisoners."

"Thank you, Commander. Carla, next meeting drag Eamon's butt in here with you."

She grinned at that. "Yes Ma'am. I'll inform the Chief of Medical Research that his presence is required at all senior staff meetings."

Everyone chuckled at that, and the captain turned to Linsey. "Alien communications?"

Linsey smiled as she gave her report, barely containing her excitement. "Captain, Medical got the diary for us and we're actually beginning to make headway. The alien language seems to be quite musical, and by a lucky chance, SUVI 18 was able to hit a note that made the tablet do several interesting things."

"Good news indeed, Linsey. Let me know the instant you crack it."

"Yes Ma'am."

"All right people, I guess it's my turn for a report now. I know you're all curious as to why I've held Reacher in place instead of proceeding on to the next planet. Here's my reasoning.

"Amanda brought us a damaged ship, and with luck, we'll soon be able to safely investigate it. It was found on a planet that may hold a great deal more salvage. Once we can understand the language we'll be in a better position to decide what to do next, go back for more salvage or continue on.

"Also, we've had a few plots and uprising attempts quelled, as well as some dangerous men brought to justice. They've been sentenced to exile, but at the moment, the nearest planet we're aware of that they could survive on is Elysium, down in the caverns. This is another decision we have to make, do we move on, or go back and dump them off. This is now open for discussion. Options, opinions?"

Brandon Hoffman was the first to speak. "I wouldn't recommend taking them back to the caverns. If the rest of the grounders got wind that we'd turned back, they'd be afraid they were all going to be sent back. We'd have a full-scale mutiny on our hands."

The first officer was next. "Captain, we're putting those men into cryo-sleep. Once on ice they'll keep easily enough. I don't think we need to go back to Elysium. On the other hand, the possibilities of what we could salvage/learn on the frost world are truly intriguing.

"From what I understand that world suffered a doomsday event. Amanda found dead bodies and a broken ship. I'm willing to bet there are more salvageable ships there, and perhaps even more alien tech. I'd truly love to look that situation over."

Suvi-jean smiled at that. "Commander Volkov, are you volunteering to take command of Explorer Two?"

"Explorer Two is finished?"

"It soon will be," sighed the Chief Engineer. "Since the captain pulled everybody off the alien tech, I had to have something to keep them busy. Yes, we can have her ready in a couple of days. Actually, I'd like to re-name this ship, she's not really an explorer, she's a salvage ship, designed to go after anything exciting Explorer One might find."

Suvi-jean was grinning now. "What shall we name her, Moira?"

"How about Recovery One?"

"Works for me, I like it. So, she's ready to fly?"

"Just a couple more days to finish running tests and take a short flight then she'll be ready for her first mission. Do we have a mission?"

"You tell me. What do you know of their metals, instruments, propulsion systems, are these things worth exploring?"

"I like their metal, it appears to be lighter and stronger than ours, plus, considering how long it's been lying about, it seems durable enough. I won't know much about the rest until Linsey cracks the language barrier, but I'd guess it'll be well worth going back for a look. In fact, I'd love to see if we can repair and fly one of their ships."

"Well, Olga, want your own ship or not?"

Olga Volkov laughed at that. "Sure, Jeannie, sounds like fun. You'll need someone to fill in while I'm off the Reacher."

"Understood. Amanda the beautiful, want the job?"

Amanda smiled. "Thank you, Captain, but no. Remember what happened the last time I got a new job. Perhaps the Chief of Security?"

"Brandon?"

"Why not. Okay, Jeannie, I'll be your back up First Officer. I'll need to promote Sheila and Jake."

"Sheila and Jake?"

"Sheila will need to take my place and she'll want Jake as her Second."

"Do it, Brandon. Now, if there's nothing further, we can shoo Linsey back to work. We need that language and fast."

"Then with your permission, Captain, I'll be about the task," smiled Linsey. The captain nodded, and she fairly danced from the room in her hurry to get back to her office and the puzzling diary that awaited there.

* * * * *

Linsey arrived at her office to find SUVI 18 pacing about, her eyes glowing amber. "Eighteen, what is it?"

For an answer, Eighteen turned to the big screen attached to the diary and made a sound followed by a musical note and another sound. <*Diary, awaken.*> The screen suddenly lit up with row upon row of symbols. <*Repeat the last paragraph.*> Obediently, the machine responded and the room was suddenly filled with a soft feminine voice speaking and singing at once.

"Oh my god, you did it," squealed Linsey as she seized Eighteen in a bear hug and swung her around and around.

"You are pleased?" asked Eighteen as she was returned to her feet. Her eyes were wide open and glowing amber. She was trembling with the effort it had taken to keep from killing Linsey for grabbing her.

Startled, Linsey stepped back and made eye contact with Eighteen. "Eighteen, oh god, I'm so sorry, I didn't mean ... I didn't think, I was just so happy and excited that you solved it that I ..."

"Linsey, stop. You didn't hurt me, just nearly scared me to death. That was an expression of joy?"

"Oh yes indeed it was. I'm so sorry. I know ..."

"Then do it again."

"What?"

"You heard me, do it again. This time I'll be expecting it."

"Oh god, Eighteen, I'm so sorry. How about I just hug you?"

"That would be acceptable," replied Eighteen, smiling at last.

Linsey took the smaller woman in her arms and held her gently. "Eighteen, I'm so terribly sorry for that. Please forgive me."

SUVI 18 returned the hug. "That natural exuberance of yours will either be the death of me or cure me of my fears." She tightened her arms around Linsey. "You're forgiven, Linsey, and I have survived. Now stop this, you have work to do. We'll go binge on desserts at the end of shift."

"Oh yeah, count on that, sweet sister. Now show me what you did here."

"I have it on this device. The symbol is followed by the note then the next symbol. I've managed to translate a few words, but no more."

"Teach them to me, teach me now." Eighteen was grinning as she began.

* * * * *

Suvi-jean and her friends were gathered at the captain's table when Linsey and Eighteen arrived at the mess hall. At a signal from Suvi-jean they quickly joined them. "I see by the excitement on Linsey's face, you've made progress, Eighteen."

"We have, Captain. Show her, Linsey."

"Yes Ma'am," grinned Linsey as she set the diary on the table and spoke. *<Diary awaken. Repeat the last paragraph.>*

The others were amazed as the tablet began to speak with a soft feminine voice. The language was musical and pleasant to listen to. "Linsey, you two are utterly amazing, you've cracked it."

"Not quite yet, Captain. Eighteen first got the key to activate it, then she taught me. However, we're not quite there yet. We've made a giant leap forward, but still have a long way to go."

"Explain."

"There's still much we don't understand, but we now have a native speaker to listen to, so we can get the inflections right. We can now activate the diary, and the star chart you found on Elysium."

SUVI 18 spoke up. "Captain, we believe their systems are voice activated. Therefore, we concluded the salvaged ship was trying to escape the planet. She was probably trying to shoot any debris that came close. That's why that man was able to fire the weapon, the system was already active. We need to learn more, then go in and shut down all systems before further investigation happens."

"Good thinking. Linsey, what's your best guess for a timeline?"

"Captain, yesterday I might have said probably months or never, but with Eighteen's breakthrough, give us a couple more days and we could be working on full translation programs for Engineering. We should be ready then to start training people to speak basic commands. <*Diary, sleep.*> The tablet chirped a response then went dark.

Amanda grinned as she spoke to Linsey. "So, just how much of that diary have you read?"

"Not nearly enough, and yet, enough to feel completely intrusive." She was blushing and looking at her plate. "There's a lot of emotion poured into that diary, and listening to it is tormenting my poor Eighteen."

Jeannie raised an eyebrow at SUVI 18. "Talk to me, Eighteen. Are you all right? Can you do this?"

"I am, and I can, Five. Linsey keeps me grounded when it gets too strong. As near as we can understand, the one who wrote this was the daughter of a powerful leader. She fell in love with a serving girl, and he found out about it, sentenced the serving girl to death. Our writer took her lover and fled to the colonies on the outer edge of the Empire.

"Captain, I get a sense that these people weren't just explorers and colonizers, I think they were a warrior society as well."

"I'm not surprised," sighed Jeannie. "People colonize for one of two reasons, either they come conquering to steal resources, or they're driven by the need to survive as our own people were.

"This is good work, far more than I dared to hope for. Congratulations, ladies. I'm so thrilled with your success."

"It was Eighteen's success, Captain. She's the one who figured it out. She should hold the rank, be your communications officer."

SUVI 18 gently patted Linsey's hand. "No, Linsey. I stumbled on a word, you took that to the next level, a place I would never have reached. I am SUVI, I need no rank, no title other than my name. We SUVI met and agreed we would not hold rank unless it is absolutely vital.

"SUVI 5 is the captain, and thus speaks for us all. Linsey, we were slaves, and as such we have a natural aversion to orders, either taking or giving. We strive to serve the greater good of the many without that."

"But ..."

"Twenty."

At that spoken word Linsey stared wide eyed at Eighteen then nodded and lowered her eyes. Eighteen reached over to gently pat her hand. Seeing the captain's raised eyebrow, she smiled and explained.

"Linsey's mind works much like a SUVI's, and so I called her SUVI 20 when we were first working together. Occasionally her exuberance gets the best of her, so we agreed that, should I call her Twenty, she would stop speaking and think through the conversation before proceeding.

"Now, my delightful SUVI 20, hear me. You know full well what happens to me, how easily I get overwhelmed. I cannot hold rank, or be in command, it would destroy me. You handle it with ease, the task is yours. I'll help and support you wherever I can, but you're the ranking officer. Are we clear on this?"

Linsey sighed and lightly squeezed Eighteen's hand. "Yes ma'am, very clear." Suvi-jean smiled and winked at Amanda.

Chapter #6

Glimmers of Hope

It was three days after Linsey's little demonstration that the captain received the call. "Sub-Commander da Silva to the captain."

"Sorenson here, Linsey. What's the good word?"

"Eighteen and I are ready to go into the salvaged ship, Captain."

"Wait for me, I'll have Engineering and Medical on standby."

SUVI 18 was trying to calm an excited Linsey when the captain arrived, accompanied by the Chief Engineer and two medics. "All right, Linsey, this is your baby. Take the lead."

Linsey nodded then turned to the silent spaceship. "These ships are operated by artificial intelligence, Captain. I'll have to talk him into working with us." The captain nodded, and Linsey began. <Ship, awaken."> There was a soft hum and the interior lights came on.

A strong male sounding voice replied. <Scout ship 87643 responding. Ship damaged, unable to fly.>

The tablet in Eighteen's hand translated as Linsey interacted with the ship. <Ship, systems report.>

<Engines offline, but repairable, life support offline, small weapons functional, ion cannon beyond repair. Crew missing. Where is captain Exran?>

<Exran and crew have been relieved. I am Captain Linsey da Silva. You will respond to me.>

<Captain da Silva and companions are of an unknown species to the Empire. How has Captain da Silva obtained command?>

<Ship was damaged. Much time has passed. The builders are no more. Ship was found on a barren planet, retrieved. Our species wants to repair Ship, adopt.>

There was a long moment before she got a response. <Ship acknowledges Captain da Silva. Ship will respond. Orders?>

<Ship needs repairs. Take all weapons offline.>

<Ship has complied. Weapons offline. Further orders?>

<This is Chief Engineer Duncan. She will study, explore all systems, all information, effect repairs. Comply.>

<Ship accepts Engineer Duncan. Captain da Silva, suggestion.>

<Speak.>

<Ship can learn new language faster.>

<Understood. Ship's information receivers incompatible with ours.>

<Understood. Ship will assimilate new language as audio presents.>

<Accepted. Commander Duncan will speak now.> "All yours, Commander Duncan. Speak into this device and it should translate for you, in theory."

Moira accepted the device Linsey passed to her, arching an eyebrow at her. <Ship, display propulsion schematic.>

<Approach engineering station display.> Moira looked around and saw a panel flashing light. She looked at the display and shook her head. "All right, Linsey, how do I read this."

<Perhaps Engineer Duncan would prefer audio display.>

Moira saw Linsey nod, so she agreed. The ship began to speak and the unit in her hand began to translate. Smiling, the others withdrew, leaving her to it.

* * * * *

While the Chief Engineer got lost in alien schematics, the Captain and the others returned to the medical bay. They found Carla tending to the two alien bodies which had now returned to full scale. "Carla?"

"Captain, this is the craziest thing. Just as I was arriving this morning we got a beep."

"A beep?"

"Once I had Linsey's diary for her I slowed down the thawing process. I was afraid they might begin to deteriorate or something, so I slowed it down. They reached room temp last night, and this morning their internal temperature had climbed higher on its own.

"I tried to re-hydrate them as you wanted, but they really didn't need much. In truth, all I gave them was some saline to help fill them out. We've had them hooked to monitors, and this morning we got a beep. It's not much, but their skin is beginning to react."

"So they're alive?"

"Oh, I won't go that far, but their skin is reacting. I have no idea if we can go any further or not. Want to see them?"

"Yes indeed."

"Right this way." She led them to a different room where the lovers still lay side by side, but now looked very different. The aliens had round cherubic faces, small mouths with full lips, thin straight noses, and large round ears that fit close to the skull. Like humans, they had two arms, and two legs. Each arm had a hand with four fingers and two thumbs. The delicate feet had six toes each, but no thumbs. The large eyes were closed in repose.

"Can you revive them, Carla?"

"Doubt it, but who knows. They've warmed up enough, and they have similar organs to ours. What the hell, want to give it a shot?"

"Oh, you know I do," grinned Suvi-jean.

"Okay then, stand back. Ellen, give me a hand here."

Another medic stepped in to help her, they charged up the pads then shocked the first woman, the one who'd written the diary. On the third try they actually got a response. The fourth hit gave them a slow heartbeat.

Wide eyed, Carla moved the machine away. "I want this woman monitored every minute of every day. Help me separate them now. Bring up another bed for the second one, let's see if we can get a spark from her too. Everybody else, out."

The others stepped out of the room and waited. Carla soon joined them. "Jeannie, I have no idea at all why any of that worked, I don't. By all the laws of nature and reason it shouldn't have."

"But?"

"But it did, must be something about their physiology that made it possible. We've got a heartbeat from both of them. Now we have to monitor closely and hope the rest of their organs respond as well. I have no idea at all what some of them are. Also, we don't have any brain activity as yet. Linsey, could you do me a favor?"

"Sure. What do you need?"

"Any medical information from that magic ship of yours would be a start, anything at all you can get me."

"On it. Come on, Eighteen, let's go see what we can scare up."

"And I'll clear out so you can work," smiled Suvi-jean.

* * * * *

When they arrived back at the ship Linsey was greeted in English. "Ship recognizes Sub-Commander da Silva."

"Ship, you've assimilated our language."

"Correct."

"You are also aware I am not your new captain."

"Sub-Commander da Silva is in charge of all things Ship, therefore, there was no deception. What was done was necessary for Ship to accept repairs. Sub-Commander da Silva arrives with a request?"

"Yes. We have two people of the builder species on the Reacher. We're trying to revive them. I need all the medical information you have."

"Commander Duncan has adjusted information device connections. Approach medical panel and attach a receiving device. Do you wish the information in your own language?"

"Yes, Ship. That is preferred." Linsey attached the info tablet, there was a flash of light on the panel, then a moment later the light faded.

"All available medical information has been successfully copied to the information unit."

"Excellent. Thank you Ship."

"You are welcome, Sub-Commander da Silva."

Linsey took the tablet and raced away, SUVI 18 close behind her. She was puffing as she entered the infirmary and passed the tablet to Carla. "Wow, that was fast."

"We aim to please. We'll let you work now, good luck with the revival."

"Thanks, I'll need it."

* * * * *

Three days later the captain called a senior staff meeting. They gathered and began the reports. "Engineering is happy," grinned Moira Duncan. "Recovery One is online and ready for her first mission. Ship 87643 has shifted to English and that's making things a lot easier. We've reached the point where we need more of their metals, and it would be nice to find a few spare parts."

Suvi-jean grinned at that. "So, are you suggesting I send Captain Volkov and her new ship back for a salvage mission?"

Moira matched her grin. "Aye, Captain. That is indeed what I'm suggesting."

"Olga, have you picked your crew yet?"

"I have, Captain. I even pulled a certain relative of yours out of retirement for a first officer, with your permission, of course."

"Granted, but please don't let him take that old speeder with him. He'll break his neck with that thing. Medical, how are our passengers doing?"

"They're both breathing on their own, Captain, and we're getting quite a bit of brain activity from Morthel, but not so much yet from Antha."

"Carla, where did those names come from?"

"Linsey pulled them from the diary."

"Linsey?"

"Okay, I'll admit we've been hanging around medical lately. Since Ship learned English there's nothing for us to do there, but when Morthel awakens she'll be frightened and will need someone who can explain to her what's going on.

"Captain, can you tell us what you plan to do with them?"

The room went quiet at that. Suvi-jean smiled and relaxed back in her chair. "If either of them revives they will be offered a place on the Reacher. If they prefer to leave then we'll try to get Ship ready to carry them away, but I hope they'll stay.

"These people have a wealth of information we could use, plus, if we ever encounter their species it would be an advantage to have a few of them on our crew."

"So you plan to offer them sanctuary, not study them?"

"Yes, Eamon, assuming they actually do revive, they'll be treated as equals, offered a place here with us, or helped to go on their way. These people are alive, they're not lab specimens."

"I'm relieved to hear you say that, Captain."

"Eamon, I'm not the enemy here, neither am I Farouk Bladon."

"I know, Jeannie, I know. I thought long and hard about what happened here at that last meeting I attended. I realize now your SUVI brain works differently, and I responded as though I had been attacked, was being singled out for censure. That wasn't true, was it? You were just stating the facts and pointing out the obvious that had completely escaped me.

"On a brighter note, with the information Linsey got for Carla, we've put our heads together and I believe we can revive Morthel at least, maybe Antha as well."

Suvi-jean sat quietly for a long moment. "How long before you know?"

"Soon," replied Carla. "If all goes well we'll try to revive Morthel this afternoon."

The captain sat lost in thought. Amanda patted her hand. "Jeannie."

"Oh, sorry. Do it, people. Olga, hold off on your launch. If we can revive one of them perhaps we can revive more. I don't want to steal space in your cargo hold, so I'll send the Explorer with you to look for more intact bodies. If we can save some of these people, we should make every effort to do so."

"Why?"

"Brandon?"

The chief of Security was grinning. "I know how your mind works, Captain. I'm just curious about your reasoning."

"They're fellow beings, and it causes no harm to us to help them. Also, they've been where we want to go. Imagine if one of them could show us where to locate the perfect planet, tell us what we'd be likely to find there. I assure you, things on Elysium would have been much different had we known of the Oraks and the virus before we landed.

"Think of it people, the wealth of helpful knowledge these people could impart to us, the time they could save us, the lives spared."

Brandon smiled even wider. "Jeannie, I never doubted you for a minute. As usual, you're two steps ahead of the rest of us. So, you're planning to take the Reacher back there?"

"I am, yes, if Carla can bring Morthel around. If we stay here, then both ships have to waste weeks ferrying salvage and bodies back here. If the Reacher is in orbit, then we save a lot of time."

"Jeannie, you know what this will do, the grounders will panic, there'll be a mutiny, or worse."

"I know, that's why I have a special task for you."

"Me?"

"Yes you, Brandon. You know who is most likely to lead the mutiny. I want you to bring me five or six of them."

"Jeannie, what are you going to do?"

"The grounders know all too well what happened on Elysium. They'll be able to see the benefits of going back to investigate if it can prevent another disaster."

"You're planning to tell them everything, try to bring them on side?"

"Yes."

Brandon grinned at her. "There's never a dull moment with you as captain. All right, Jeannie, I'll round up a few dissidents for you. Should be fun."

"All right, people, let's get to it."

As everyone left the room, Amanda took Suvi-jean by the hand. "Jeannie, honey, I've got an idea. Will you let me help here?"

"Of course, Mandy. Tell me what you've got in mind."

"It's about the grounders and how we can stop all the mutiny and such. Sweetheart, I know why you did what you did with those criminals, and I'll confess, having Lathan in cryo sleep eases my mind, but that action will cause people to become uneasy."

"Sadly, I do understand that. So, what's the solution?"

"Give me the grounders."

"Mandy?"

"Put me in charge of the grounders and grounder-crew relations. Let me deal with them first, then you can meet with them and tell them what you have in mind."

"You're serious."

"I am."

"They're all yours, sweetheart, and welcome to them."

Chapter #7

Grounders

Several people sat around a table in the smaller of the passenger mess halls. Some were advocating for a mutiny, others wanted to confront the captain, but three others suggested a more cautious approach.

Miriam Holbrooke sighed and shook her head. "You can't do it, you can't. Good god, Farouk Bladon had over sixty troops plus the SUVI and she beat them. What chance do you think you have? Come on, people, face a bit of reality here."

"Since when did you become a SUVI lover, and what do you mean, face reality?"

"Look, I've never had a problem with the SUVI, and I always believed enslaving them was a mistake."

"You never said anything."

"No I didn't, because if I had somebody would have blabbed to Farouk and I'd have been tossed out to survive on the surface. Honestly, think about the way we had to live in the caverns, is that what you really want to go back to?"

"No, I don't. So what are you suggesting?"

"I'm suggesting we try to find a way to work with the Captain, find out what she's planning, maybe even seeing if we can have a dialogue with her. Look, we all set out to establish a deep space colony, but we were all in our thirties and forties back then, and that was thirty years ago.

"Think about this. If we keep pissing her off she could dump us off someplace worse than Elysium. Personally, I'm getting too damned old to go farming on some alien planet, and so are most of the rest of us. Our younger people were either born in space of the caverns. I'm pretty sure they're happier here on the ship.

"Look at Lilly Peters, she made the effort and got herself a position on the Explorer, she's found her place."

Another man snorted. "So you want to throw away the dream and retire to be a passenger on the ship?"

"I can think of worse alternatives."

"We could take the ship, go home to Earth."

"There is no Earth to go home to."

"Do you really believe that, Miriam?"

"Actually I do. I saw old Captain Baris's face when he spoke of it." They were still at it when the Chief of Security strode through the door and approached them.

* * * * *

"Security to Captain Sorenson."

"Here, Brandon. What's up?"

"I'm here in passenger mess #3 with a group of former colonists. They're refusing to move, claiming they've done nothing wrong, and they don't believe me when I tell them you just want to talk to them."

"Order up a couple of sweet drinks, Commander Drake and I will be right there."

"Understood." Brandon Hoffman sighed and waved off his security men. "All right, people, you heard the captain, she's on her way here to talk to you. I've sent the security men away. No one here is in trouble, no one here is facing arrest at the moment. You are, however, invited to listen to the captain as she informs you of some things going on at this time that will be of great interest to you as colonists."

"Has it to do with the aliens? Is it about why we've stopped travelling toward the next planet?"

"Be patient. The captain will soon be here and, ... ah, there she comes now."

Suvi-jean and Amanda entered the mess and chose drinks then approached the group where Brandon was standing guard. "Did any of them escape, Brandon?"

He grinned. "Not a single one, Captain."

"Want to stick around for the show?"

"Do you need security?"

"Nope, not necessary."

"Then I have other tasks to occupy my day. With your permission, Captain." Jeannie nodded, and Commander Hoffman turned and walked away.

"Mind if we join you folks?"

Amanda's question jolted them out of their shock. Some of them shuffled down to give them room to sit at the long table. "Okay, I'll start. I'm Commander Amanda Drake, Head of Social Engagement and Commander of Explorer One. The captain and I have asked to meet with you for a number of reasons.

"First up, we made a mistake. We tried to integrate all the colonists with the crew of the Reacher. You folks aren't ship's crew, you're colonists, passengers, and should be treated as such.

"Having said that, any colonist is welcome to apply for a position on ship's crew, and, conversely, we hope that any crewmember who wishes to retire and join the colonists would be welcomed.

"Now we come to the second point of today's meeting. The people at this table have been noticed as natural leaders among the colonists."

"You mean the grounders," muttered one woman.

Amanda smiled as she responded. "Yeah, I'm not really liking that word, not too fond of sky-rider either. Those words separate us, make it sound like we're against each other. That's not true."

"Tell that to the three dozen men in prison."

Suvi-jean sighed and patted Amanda's hand. "Those men were all brutal criminals. They abused some members of the crew before leaving the ship originally, and the SUVI especially in the caverns. They killed dozens on the surface of the planet, and left hundreds more to die. Captain Baris, in his desire to save every breathing human still in existence, forgave them their past crimes. I didn't.

"Seriously, you all know who those men were, the things they've done. Did you truly want them left free to live among you? Many of you have felt their disdain and cruelty, deny it if you can." Only silence greeted her statement, and no one would meet her eyes. "Commander Drake, please continue."

"Thank you, Captain. As I was saying, from now on, you're the colonists, we're the crew, and we all belong on this ship until we find a suitable planet we can inhabit. Now, for today we will speak with you as leaders of the colonists. In future, we'd be happier to have the colonists elect a group of five or six people to consult with us regularly."

"Why even bother? You can do whatever you want anyway."

"Perhaps, but it's not about control. Captain Sorenson isn't Farouk Bladon, she is utterly devoted to making a better life for all of us. Here's where we start, will you help us, or will you fight us? Will you set aside old resentments and work with us for the greater good of all humans and SUVI, or will you fight us and bring about the final destruction of our entire species?

"This is in your hands now, what will you do?"

"Can I get an honest answer from the captain?"

"I know you, Miriam Holbrooke. Ask, and I will answer truthfully."

"What will you do if we oppose you?"

"I'll find a planet where you could survive then dump off the lot of you for the greater good of the many. The ship's crew outnumbers the colonists by five to one or more. The welfare of the many will outweigh the needs of the few."

"Can't blame you for that," said another. "It does make sense. So, what do you want from us?"

Amanda smiled as she replied to his question. "For today, listen to the captain, give her feedback if she asks for it, then relay what you've learned to the rest of the colonists. After that, perhaps see if you can formalize the system among the colonists, elect a few officers to bring concerns to the captain, and relay her responses back to the population.

"The senior staff already does this for the crew, that's how it works. Will you do this for us?"

"All right, we're listening."

"Captain."

"Thank you, Commander Drake. People, I'm sure you know we've come to a stop about halfway to the original target. Here's why. Before we left Elysium we found an alien colony, abandoned long before we arrived there. From that colony we acquired a star chart that we hoped would lead us to a suitable planet, one that would be more welcoming than Elysium was.

"As we journeyed toward the first likely system, we sent the Explorer off to investigate yet another planet, one too far out of the goldilocks zone to be useful to us, but marked on the alien map anyway.

"We were curious why it was marked on that chart. On that planet, Explorer's crew found a number of damaged ships, and brought one back to us for study.

"They also found two frozen aliens and brought them as well. Our medical staff has managed to partially revive those two people, and we have hopes they will awaken so we can talk to them."

"Seriously? Why?"

Suvi-jean sighed and leaned her elbows on the table as she replied. "All we've got now is that old star chart. Imagine if you will, a living guide who understands our needs, a guide who has first hand information about the planets we're likely to encounter as we continue along that path laid out by their people. Would that not be more useful?"

"Yes, Captain, it surely would. Point taken, please continue."

She smiled as she went on. "If we do manage to revive one or both of those people, they will be frightened, and alone, have no real reason to help us. We want their help and so we need to have something to offer them in return."

"You mean more than their lives?"

Amanda responded to that one. "Imagine if you will, knowing you're going to die, facing it, accepting it, and holding your dead lover to you, passing into the mystery. The next thing you know, you wake up on an alien ship, among people who look very different, speak differently, behave differently. They want your help, but they've just robbed you of your peace, and you have no idea if you can trust them, of what they will do with you once they have what they need from you."

The man smiled ruefully. "I get it. If we wake them up, we need to show good faith when we ask for help. So, Captain Sorenson, what's the plan?"

"Right now, engineering is trying to repair the alien ship. As they work on that they're learning lots of interesting things that will improve life for us, such as new and stronger metals, faster and more fuel-efficient propulsion systems, and more.

"Now, apparently, that planet suffered a catastrophic event. Something hit it unexpectedly and pushed it well out of its orbit, taking it out to where it couldn't sustain life. During that event many of the colonists perished, and a large number of ships were damaged.

"My plan is to go salvage as much as we can, find and revive as many of those people as possible, then invite them to join us in our search for a home, that or ask them to show us the way then give them their ships and wish them a happy journey.

"We've got Explorer One ready to go, and another ship, a salvage ship called Recovery One, also ready to go. I want to turn the Reacher around and go back to that frozen planet to be closer for the salvage and rescue teams.

"Now, you all have a stake in this. Options? Opinions? Suggestions?"

They all sat in a stunned silence, absorbing what the captain had said. That was the last thing they'd expected to hear. Finally, one man began to grin. "Captain Sorenson, is there any chance some of us might get a job on that salvage crew?"

"You're Chance Morita, I remember you. You were often in command of salvage crews who went to the surface to gather resources from the failed colony. You want to lead this salvage operation?"

"Oh yeah, I'd love to."

"Well, I'm not the captain of Recovery One, but I'll put in a good word for you." Smiling she reached for her comm unit. "Sorenson to Commander Volkov."

"Volkov here, Captain."

"You have your first officer, but do you have an experienced salvage leader chosen yet."

"Not yet. You have someone in mind?"

"He's from the colony, has experience in such things. Chance Morita and I have worked together before, and I trust him to do the job well."

"I'm taking three crews of four, he can lead one of them. Tell him to find his crew and meet me in the cargo bay. Volkov out."

Suvi-jean looked up and grinned. "Chance Morita, why are you still here?"

"I'm already gone." He laughed as he rose and hurried away. She smiled as she watched him go.

"Captain, are you sure about this plan?"

"The plan? Yes. Will it work? Who can say, but as far as I can see, it's our best bet. As I said before, I'm open to suggestions. If you've got a better idea, let's hear it."

"We don't SU ... sorry, Captain Sorenson, we don't," replied Miriam Holbrooke, "all we have is fear, fears and questions prompted by fears. We owe you a debt of thanks for coming here today to ease our minds. You didn't have to do that, and I for one, appreciate it and what it must have cost you."

"Miriam, we all have to let go of the past, for we cannot change it. Those others were violent men we don't want loose on the ship or the in next colony. They'll face exile when we finally settle. For now, they're out of circulation and can do no further harm. The days and ways of Farouk Bladon are gone and will not return. Help me make that happen."

"Gladly, Captain. What do you need from us?"

"Go among the colonists, allay their fears, inform them of what we're doing and why. Meet with Commander Drake every seven days, bring your concerns to her, and she in turn will bring them to me. I'll meet with you as necessary. When Commander Drake is off exploring, another from her department will meet with you, or I will personally."

The colonists thanked her again as she and Amanda rose to leave. They were barely outside the mess when Suvi-jean was hit by a stunner. Amanda was grabbed from behind and held fast as five men began to fit the groggy captain with a pain collar. "Get her in it, get her in it, she's reviving. Get her in it or we'll never see Earth again. Hit her with the stunner, hit her with the stunner."

The man pulled the trigger on the stun gun, but it didn't have the desired effect. Suvi-jean had grabbed one of the attackers and pulled him into the line of fire. She shoved his twitching body aside as the pain hit. "Get up, SUVI 5, get the hell up and do as you're told."

His eyes bugged out in horror as she screamed in rage and pain, grabbed the collar, and tore it in half. She lashed out and the man with the controller died with the jagged edge of the collar lodged in his throat. The next one took a kick to the chest that sent him flying against the wall where he slid to the floor, never to rise again.

The battle was on, but swiftly over. As the fourth body hit the floor Jeannie turned to Amanda, but she hadn't needed any help. She threw her head back, striking the man who held her on the nose. He let out a yelp and loosened his grip. Amanda stomped down hard on his foot and he howled in pain as he released her. She spun and grabbed his hair then jerked his head down into her knee which was speeding up to meet his face. He fell to the deck unconscious.

The second man had come at Jeannie again, but he now lay dead on the floor. Amanda stepped past the man she'd felled to sweep Jeannie into her arms. They looked to see the last man being held down by three of the people they'd spoken with at the table. "Security is on the way. Captain, we had nothing to do with this, I swear it."

"I believe you, Miriam."

"I promise I'll personally put a stop to any more of this stupidity," growled Miriam. "We're never going back to that way of life again."

Suvi-jean nodded as Jake and three others came pounding along the corridor. "Jeannie!"

"Jake, easy, we're all right. These men jumped me and put a pain collar on me. I tore it off and killed four in the fight, Mandy brought down one and these good people got the last one."

"So that's four for the morgue and two for the cryo beds?"

"We probably should give them a trial."

"To hell with that, Captain," said Miriam. "Put 'em in the freezer and be rid of them. I promise you, we'll root out any more of these fools and drag their sorry asses to you."

"Find them, Miriam, give them to security, they'll deal with them. Ah to hell with it, they're all yours, Jake, you deal with them. Come on, Mandy, we'll go to the infirmary and get you checked out."

"I'm good, honey. It's you I'm worried about. Come on, let's go see Carla."

* * * * *

Jake and his fellow Security officer herded the two hapless men into the area where Dr. Reilly was checking the readings on the already occupied cryo beds. "Ensign White?"

"Two more volunteers for cryo sleep, Commander."

"Now wait, we didn't volunteer for ..."

"Shut the hell up, you. You men attacked the captain and tried to put her in a pain collar. She killed four of you. Consider yourselves lucky you survived."

"We're entitled to a trial, we ..."

"You're entitled to nothing. The Reacher is the last ship in existence, she is governed by the captain, a woman you attacked. You have two options. One, accept the cryo sleep and the exile that follows when we find a planet. Two, you can walk the plank, also known as an instant transport off the ship into space without a spacesuit. Choose wisely."

The two men shrank away from him, moving closer to Dr. Reilly. "They attacked Jeannie?"

"Yep, and she's got the burns on her neck from the collar to prove it. She's probably next door getting patched up right now if you want to confirm."

"There's no need. You idiots actually attacked the captain? Roll up your sleeves and get into that capsule. Mr. White, did Jeannie order you to bring them right here?"

"She wanted to give them a trial."

"But you don't."

"Nope, waste of time and resources. Even the grounders there helped the captain and suggested skipping the trial."

"I see. You're right, a waste of time and resources. You were never here; we had no such conversation." Jake grinned and left the area as Eamon Reilly lowered the transparent lid on the capsule that held the last man. "What's two or three more, really," he muttered to himself.

Chapter #8

Awakening

Carla finished checking Amanda and smiled. "You're good, Mandy. Now, Jeannie, you've got a few burn marks on your neck. What happened?" Amanda explained what had happened as Carla worked, soothing the burns, and checking for further injuries. Suddenly there was the sound of alarms and a high-pitched screaming from another room. Carla fled with Jeannie and Amanda close behind.

They burst into the room where the two alien women were being treated to find one of them hovering over the sleeping form of the second, screaming in terror and trying to fend off the medical personnel. A nurse was trying to calm her, but she couldn't understand what he was saying. "Everybody get back," barked Carla. "Somebody get Linsey da Silva in here now."

Jeannie grabbed her comm. "Sub-Commander da Silva to the medical bay, your patient is awake."

In a few short moments Linsey and Eighteen arrived. "Everybody out, we've got this." Everybody stepped out of the room. The woman was still trying to protect her companion yet moaning and wailing in fear herself. Eighteen grabbed Linsey's hand tightly. "Stay with me, Eighteen, I need you. What is she feeling?"

"Terror, blind terror, yet protectiveness of the other."

"Got it. Go to the Captain now."

"No, I'll stay with you. I can do this, Linsey, I can help you."

"Good." Linsey wasn't moving closer, nor even looking at the two alien women. That puzzled Morthel and her screams dropped to whimpers. *<Morthel, you must calm down. You must hear me.>*

This startled the woman out of her panic. She tilted her head as though trying to understand. *<What did you say?>*

<I said you must calm down. We're not trying to hurt you; we're trying to help you.>

<Your accent is terrible, difficult to understand. Where are you from? Where did you learn to speak?">

<We found you on a frozen world. I used your diary to learn your language as best I could. Morthel, please let us help you.>

Eighteen gently squeezed Linsey's hand. "Keep going, she's calming down."

<Morthel, we know you're frightened. Please let us help you, help Antha.>

The look of fear began to return and Eighteen gently squeezed Linsey's hand again. *<What do you want me to do?>*

<Come over here with me and Eighteen so our medical people can help Antha.>

<My beloved Antha. She perished; I held her as she passed. Can you truly return her to me?>

<I can't say for certain, but we will surely try. Touch her, she is warm and breathing on her own. There is some brain activity. Please let us try.>

<Very well, if you and your beloved promise your people will help her, I will permit it. Is it safe for me to touch you and your beloved companion? It is a custom of our kind when we greet new people.>

<We have a similar custom; you may touch me.>

<And your beloved companion?>

"Eighteen?" She nodded so Linsey turned back to Morthel. *<The one I cherish most will accept the touch of friendship.>*

"We need to talk," came Eighteen's whisper in her ear. It was followed by a gentle squeeze of the hand.

Linsey returned the pressure on her fingers, never taking her eyes off Morthel. The tiny woman approached slowly and extended her hands, lightly griping Linsey on the shoulders, then reaching up to touch her forehead to Linsey's. *<I am Morthel, thirty-seventh daughter of the most noble Gyliar of Ekdrin Clan.>*

<I am Sub-Commander Linsey da Silva of the spaceship Reacher. Call me Linsey.>

<Thank you, Linsey, speak to me as Morthel.>

She released Linsey's shoulders and stepped to Eighteen. As she reached for her she stopped. *<The touch of another distresses you. I will refrain.>* Eighteen shook her head then gently gripped Morthel's shoulders and brought her forehead to the alien girl's. Morthel lightly gripped her shoulders as well. *"You are the same species as Linsey, and yet not the same. You have suffered greatly but managed to survive. Your strength and courage are to be admired. You may address me as Morthel.>*

<Linsey is human. I am part human and part something else. We are called SUVI. You may call me Eighteen.>

While the formal greetings were going on Carla and others were working frantically on Antha. As Eighteen released Morthel's shoulders they heard a soft groan behind them. Morthel spun around to see Antha struggling to sit up. She leaped to her side and, chattering to her so fast Linsey couldn't follow, gently held her and helped to sit. The others drew back to give them room.

<Oh my beloved Antha, you're alive.>

<Am I? Are you certain?>

With tears of joy Morthel gently hugged her lover. *<Yes, my most cherished, I'm quite certain.>*

<But the ground leaped up, the air burned, then cold, so cold, hard to breathe. Did I fall asleep in the cold?>

<Yes, my beloved, we both did, but our new friends have awakened us.>

<Morthel, the disaster, we should have died. How could we have survived?"

<I have no idea, sweet Antha. Perhaps Linsey can tell us.>

At that point Suvi-jean returned. "Carla, how are our passengers doing?"

"Jeannie, I have no real idea at all why, but they've revived, both of them. Linsey seems to be making headway in calming things down, so I recommend we back off and let her work."

"Agreed. Linsey."

Morthel caught how swiftly everyone responded to this stranger. There was no doubt this was the one in command. She watched as Linsey spoke with her.

"Captain?"

"Can you make yourself understood?"

"Yes, Captain. Morthel says I have a terrible accent, but she can understand me."

That brought a smile and a chuckle from the captain. "Linsey, do your best to put them at ease and reassure them they won't be harmed. Tell them we're going back to the planet to see if we can find and revive more of their people. Do what you can to help Carla meet their needs. I'll check in again in the morning."

Morthel spoke softly as they watched Suvi-jean and Amanda walk away. <*That one exudes a tightly controlled power. She is in command here?*>

<*She's the captain, our commander. It was she who ordered you revived.*>

<*A female in command, such a thing could never be imagined in the Empire. I must be careful how I speak when I thank her. Will you teach me how to do this, Linsey?*>

<*Of course. I will speak to her and ask her to talk with you.*>

* * * * *

Eventually Linsey and Eighteen left to allow Morthel and Antha some rest and time alone together. As they walked back toward the office, Linsey spoke softly. "Eighteen, you're not going to beat me up, are you?"

"Twenty."

Linsey swallowed hard and remained silent. Eighteen took her hand and led her back to the office where she closed and locked the door behind them. She turned to take Linsey gently by the shoulders. "Hug me."

Linsey was more than eager to comply with that wish. She held the small woman gently to her and sighed. "Please don't beat me up."

"Linsey, you must know I would never harm you, or is that a metaphor for being angry?"

"Yeah, that."

"I'm not angry with you, just confused, and hopeful. When you spoke with Morthel, you deliberately called me your most cherished. I can feel the warmth you have for me, and I feel the same for you. I truly need to know your thoughts, your desires. There is so much you don't know, couldn't possibly understand, ..."

"Twenty."

"What?"

"Shut up, Eighteen." Linsey gently pulled her closer and kissed her lips softly. Eighteen stiffened at first, then gave a soft moan that was part sob as she melted into Linsey's arms. "Eighteen, my most cherished, use that magic you have to feel my love for you. I want you beside me forever. I don't need to know it all, love, and I know I'll never truly understand, but I'll try.

"My thoughts? I love you and want you. I want us to be together forever. My desires? We've got a lifetime to explore some of that."

"Twenty. Just shut up and kiss me again, I liked that." Linsey was more than happy to oblige.

They spent the night in Linsey's quarters where Eighteen faced a lot of old demons and experienced a joy she could never have imagined. She drifted off to sleep cuddled into Linsey's arms feeling safe and loved. She softly wept for the pure overwhelming joy of it.

* * * * *

The next morning the Captain called a meeting of the senior staff. She was wearing a scarf to cover the bandages over the burns on her neck. When all were assembled, she spoke. "People, yesterday I and Commander Drake were attacked by a number of former colonists. Of that group, only two survived. I left them in the hands of Security. Eamon, did Jake bring them to you?"

"He did. He offered them the cryo sleep or a quick trip outside the ship. I'll wake them up for a trial if you insist."

"No, leave them there. They can have a trial once we locate a new planet for a home. For now, they're out of the way.

"On a brighter note, Amanda had a productive meeting with the colonists, and I believe they're onside now. Things are looking up there. Carla, how are things going with our passengers?"

"They're both awake and doing fine, Captain. I have no idea how or why, but they're awake and appear to be healthy. Linsey's been talking to them and they're calming down."

"Linsey?"

"Captain, they're trying to absorb what all has happened to them, how long they've been frozen. I've learned a lot about their society, the one they were in at the end as well as the one they fled from."

"What can you tell us?"

"Morthel was a younger daughter of a highly positioned noble, her mother being a member of the extended royal family. The Empire was utterly male dominant, women little more than chattel. Morthel and Antha joined a faction of rebels who smuggled them out of the empire and helped settle them on that planet.

"It seems the rebels, who believed in equality, were pretty much ignored as long as they stayed far away from the center of the Empire. The planet where we found them was the second last one in the rebel chain. Elysium would have been the last outpost in that chain.

"Morthel warns that if we continue to back track them we could bump into the Empire. Not something we want to do."

"Oh, why not?"

"We would be attacked instantly and conquered, used as slave labor on a mining world. Captain, Morthel believes it wasn't a rogue asteroid that hit her planet. She believes it was an Imperial warship. They had weapons with that kind of power and often used them. An asteroid would have been seen in plenty of time for a full evacuation. These folks barely got two thirds of their people off planet in time."

Suvi-jean sat lost in thought and no one disturbed her. Finally she sighed and brought her attention back to the room, her eyes slowly fading from amber back to their natural green. "It took humans less than twenty thousand years to go from hunter gatherers to utterly destroying themselves with the power of the weapons they invented.

"These people have been out of circulation for a lot longer than that. Speculate, people. What are the chances that empire has survived to this day?"

It was Brandon who spoke first. "I'd say that one's long gone, Captain. Every empire ever known self-destructed in the end. I guess the question is, have others risen in their place, is one in existence now with the same capabilities?"

"All good questions, Brandon. Sadly, we have no answers at this time. Opinions? Options?"

"Captain, let's not pick a fight with an empire that may or may not exist. Let's focus on the task at hand."

"Thank you, Olga, I'm in full agreement there. First I want to get the salvage operation going, save what we can use, revive more people if we can, but gather as many resources and as much information as that planet will yield up. With any luck we'll get a better star chart and someone who can read it, help to point the way so we can avoid that Empire.

"Commander Jones, what's our progress?"

"We'll reach planetary orbit late tomorrow, Captain."

"Excellent. Moira, how are those engine modifications holding up?"

"Ah, Jeannie, the engines are purring away quite happily. We're getting sixty per cent more speed and using half the fuel, plus the engines aren't working as hard to do it. Better yet, there's still more to learn. For an empire to operate efficiently on an interstellar basis, they had to have had far superior engines."

"Now, that is good news. People, our prospects seem to be improving. So, is there any further business?"

"If I may, Captain."

"What is it, Linsey?"

"Morthel would like to formally thank you and the senior staff for her rescue, and especially for reviving Antha. May I bring her in?"

"Of course."

"Thank you, Captain." Linsey reached for her comm. "Linsey to SUVI 18."

"Here."

"The captain says it's a go. Bring the girls to the captain's briefing room."

"On our way."

A few moments later there was a soft tap at the door, then at the captain's call, Eighteen led the two aliens into the room. They looked so small, like children, in the oversized chairs. Jeannie nodded and at Linsey's whispered word, Morthel rose, holding a tablet in her hand. When she spoke, the tablet translated for her.

"Captain Sorenson, leaders of the Reacher, I am Morthel. Linsey said to dispense with titles, and so I shall. Captain, I have no voice to express my joy at suddenly returning to awareness to find myself safe on a ship with my beloved Antha at my side. The kindness and generosity of your people overwhelms me."

She reached for Antha's hand then went on. "What you wonderful people have given me is beyond imagining. Linsey has told me of your quest, and of how you found us, more she has tried to explain how long we were frozen on that planet, but the mind rebels at trying to encompass that.

"Captain Sorenson, we are in your debt. What can we do to repay you, to aid you in your quest?"

"Will that tablet translate my words to her?" As Jeannie finished speaking the tablet sang in Morthel's language. She smiled and nodded eagerly. "Excellent. Morthel, the knowledge gained from your diary made it possible for Linsey to activate the damaged ship we found. We have learned much from this, and as a result we now have faster engines, stronger metals, and more.

"We are well compensated, but if you truly want to help us, we would be grateful for the assistance."

"We will be happy to contribute in any way we can, Captain. However, this language devise Linsey has created is useful, but there is a much better way. She tells me the salvaged ship has a functioning core, and that it has already mastered your manner of speech. If the core is willing, we can learn your language in a matter of hours, thus making it easier for us to communicate. Will you permit this?"

"I will. Linsey, take Morthel and Antha to the ship and see what can be done with this. All right, people, we'll meet here again tomorrow morning to get organized." With that she rose and left the room.

* * * * *

"Greetings, Sub-Commander da Silva. You have two Earalith with you. Are you passing over command?"

"I greet you, Ship. No, for now I retain my command. However, these people have a request, will you hear them?"

"Of course. Lady Morthel, Mistress Antha, you are recognized."

It was Morthel who responded. <We have met before, Ship?>

<Ship was privileged to carry you from space to the colony below upon your arrival at planet Nithon.>

<It was a gentle landing and I remember it well. Ship, Antha and I have a great need to learn the language of our saviors. Will you aid us?>

<Ship will comply with Sub-Commander da Silva's permission.>

Linsey nodded, smiling. <Granted, Ship.>

<Lady Morthel, approach the communication station, apply the helmet of learning.>

Antha stood back beside Linsey, watching as Morthel approached the blinking light. She touched a panel and it popped open. Morthel withdrew a cap with several wires attached and pulled it on. After pressing it snugly onto her head she spoke. <Please proceed, Ship.>

Her eyes rolled back and she grasped the edge of the rail to steady herself. There were a few moments of disorientation, then a steady stream of images flowed into her mind. Slowly Morthel became aware of sounds accompanying the images. The sounds increased in speed and cadence to become words, sentences, and more. She listened to recorded conversations and began to understand them.

Slowly the process slowed down and Morthel became aware of the soft voices of the crew nearby. She smiled with delight as she realized she could understand them. Suddenly the ship was talking to her, demanding responses. It took a while for her voice to adjust to making the new sounds, but she got it, the rhythm of it.

The ship went silent and she removed the cap from her head and turned. Linsey was sprawled in the captain's chair and Antha was leaning against a control panel as was Eighteen. They were chatting and the language, her own language, sounded strange to her for a few moments.

Morthel stepped towards them. "Sub-Commander Linsey da Silva, I greet you in English. At least, I hope that's what I did."

Linsey laughed with delight. "Yes. Friend Morthel, you did indeed greet me in English. Antha's turn now?"

"Sadly, that won't be possible."

"Why not?"

"My beloved Antha is of a much lower caste, and as such will be forbidden."

"We'll see about that. Ship."

"Speak, Sub-Commander."

"I require Lady Morthel's companion, Antha, to learn my language. Will you help me?"

"It is forbidden for Ship to obey or aid a member of the Krill class in any way."

"Even under battle conditions?"

"Ship does not understand."

"I am Linsey da Silva, Commander of Ship 87643, Ship is damaged, unable to fly or self-repair. Antha has information vital to my ability to bring help to repair Ship. In this time of emergency, I command Ship 87643 to override original programming in this case. I must be able to communicate with Antha in my own language."

"There is no protocol for such action."

"Create protocol, Linsey 0123, any and all members of the species Earalith are required to have access to the English language."

She could have sworn there was amusement in the ship's reply. "Protocol created, Sub-Commander da Silva. Instruct Antha to approach the communications panel." Linsey grinned and nodded to Morthel who gently urged Antha to the panel and helped her into the helmet.

Wide-eyed and unsure, Antha gave Ship the go-ahead. She gasped as her awareness shifted. A long wait later, she removed the helmet and turned to her companions. "That was utterly amazing." With a squeal of delight, Morthel swept her into loving arms and hugged her tightly.

"Ship warns that the new language must be practiced daily for a time or it could be lost."

"Thank you, Ship, I promise I'll make sure they practice each day."

"Sub-Commander da Silva, Ship has an enquiry."

"What is it, Ship?"

"You always speak to Ship as you would to an equal of your own species. This is not necessary. Ship is a tool, a machine to be used as needed, to be instructed, to be assigned tasks. Why do you do this?"

"I do this because Ship is an intelligent being, capable of independent thought, of making decisions independently of prior instruction. Ship is a living entity, a living, thinking, being under my command. I speak as I do because I respect Ship. Ship is my friend."

"What you say is completely foreign to Ship's prior experience. Ship is not a being, Ship is a thing, a tool, therefore what you say is not possible."

"Ship is indeed a being, different from me, just as Lady Morthel is different from me, and yet still a living being. Ship is a living being, Ship is my friend."

"I do not understand. I must consider what you have said carefully."

"Until we meet again, Friend Ship." Grinning, Linsey led her companions away.

"Friendship, a play on words to express pleasure. Until we meet again, Captain da Silva." Linsey was still chuckling as they walked away.

Morthel looked puzzled. "Linsey, your rank is Sub-Commander, and Ship 87643 knows this. Why did it call you Captain?"

"When we first awakened Ship, he wanted to know where his captain was, and what was going on. He was quite suspicious. I told him I was Captain da Silva, his new captain. He later learned the truth of his situation, and that I am actually still in command of all things Earalith, including ships, and he has accepted that."

"Ship expressed an idea of humor. That would not be tolerated in the empire."

"I get the sense we're quite different from that empire."

"Yes indeed, that you are, Linsey, and I for one, like the difference."

Chapter #9

Salvage

It was only slight, but everyone felt it as the great ship dropped her speed to sub-light and moved into a parking orbit around the frozen planet. "Standard orbit achieved, Captain."

"Well done, Commander Jones, I didn't feel a thing."

"Thank you, Captain."

"You have the bridge, Emmet. I'm going down to see our explorers off." He grinned as he saluted her, then she turned and left. She met her grandfather on the way to the cargo bay.

"Is that a uniform I see you in, Grandfather? Retirement a little boring?"

"Not at all. Jeannie, thank you for approving this post for me. I finally get my wish to go exploring."

"You had this planned all along, didn't you, setting me up to take the ship so you could go play."

"Jeannie Sorenson, that thought never crossed my mind."

"Ah-huh."

"It didn't, but I can't say I'm overly upset at how it's worked out."

"So I see."

"Jeannie, are you teasing me?"

"Yes. How am I doing?"

He chuckled at that. "Your technique is improving. Jeannie, I heard there was an incident a few days ago. Can I ask what happened?"

"Several men jumped us, hit me with a stunner and put a home-made pain collar around my neck, then turned it up to max. They wanted to gain control of Reacher through me." She pulled down the collar of her tunic to show him the burns on her throat.

"My god, Jeannie, what ...?"

"I tore it off and fought them. Only two of six managed to survive and they're in cryo sleep. They were part of Farouk's old security team, some of those who escaped the investigation."

"Jeannie, I swear I had no real idea what I'd done by bringing all those people up here and leaving them loose. I should have ..."

"No, Grandfather, you did no wrong, you followed your own codes of conduct, the things that make you the man you are, the grandfather I love dearly. However, I'm an entirely different being, and I know some of the things I've done disturb you. Last time we met I spoke harshly to you, and I regret that.

"I realize you're only doing your job, trying to be my mentor and my conscience. I did ask you to do this, then chewed you out for it. I apologize for that."

"No apology necessary, Jeannie. We're still trying to get to know one another. We'll get through it."

"For the greater good?" she grinned.

He laughed and gently squeezed her arm. "Yes, for the greater good."

Amanda was smiling brightly at them as they arrived. "Well, it's nice to see you two have made up."

"The family is stable once again, sweet Amanda. So, is Explorer One ready?"

"Ready and just waiting for our consultants to arrive. Ah, there they are now."

The captain turned to see the two Earalith hurrying along with Linsey and Eighteen. Olga Volkov arrived at the same time. "I'd better get busy and see to the readiness of the ship," grinned the newly commissioned first officer of Recovery One. "Don't want to disappoint the captain on the first day. So, who's with me here?"

"Eighteen and I will accompany Recovery One, Sir. Lady Morthel and Antha will be on Explorer One."

"This your idea, Linsey?"

"I'm sorry, Captain, it just ..."

"No, Linsey, relax I put you in charge of all things of an alien nature, this was your decision to make. I'm just curious about your reasoning."

"Captain, Antha was involved with many of the social activities of the community. She and Morthel will have a better idea of where we might find more people. Eighteen and I can speak Earalithian well enough to activate any functional machinery we might find, so we should be with Recovery just in case."

"Sound reasoning indeed, Linsey. All right, people, we've settled into orbit around the planet. You may launch when ready." Amanda kissed her cheek then turned to board Explorer.

As they all headed for their ships, Jeannie noticed Jake standing near. "She'll leave without you, Jake."

"I know. We agreed I should remain on the Reacher."

"Oh?"

"Explorer doesn't need security for this mission, Jeannie."

"But Reacher does?"

"You know it does."

"Still watching my back?"

"Always and forever, little sister."

"Big brother, that truly does bring me comfort. Want to join me on the bridge to watch the action?"

"Love to."

* * * * *

Recovery One slipped from the belly of the Reacher and slowly approached the daylight side of the planet. As they settled into a low orbit Commander Volkov spoke to her crew. "Attention all hands, this is Commander Volkov. We are approaching the planet Captain Sorenson has dubbed Frigid.

"Our task is to locate and recover as much useable salvage as possible. You all know your jobs, so let's make the Reacher proud. Before we get started, are there any questions?"

"Team leader three here, Commander. I have a concern."

"You're Chance Morita, yes? What is your concern, Mr. Morita?"

"Ma'am, I'm told that, aboard the Reacher, someone accidently set off a weapons system. I'm also told the alien ships are operated by an AI. More, the original builders had a male only crew aboard these ships and Sub-Commander da Silva had difficulty convincing the ship to accept her commands."

"You've done your homework, Mr. Morita, so where are you going with this?"

"Ma'am, has any male of our species been trained in that language enough to command a damaged ship to comply. I'd rather not be trying to salvage something that thinks it's under attack, especially if it's armed."

"You make a strong point, Mr. Morita. Sub-Commander da Silva is bringing each team leader a translation tablet she has created for this very purpose. She used Commander Hoffman's voice signature. The tablet will translate your words in his voice. Once the AI agrees to accept your commands you can have it power down weapons and help with its own rescue."

"Thank you, Ma'am, that's a weight off my mind."

"Excellent. Anybody else? No? All right then, let's get to it."

Recovery One dropped out of orbit and began scanning the surface of the planet, moving slowly in a steady grid pattern. "Anything, Mr. Baris?"

"Not much, Commander," replied the smiling former captain at the scanner. "We're on the damaged side, the point of original impact is right up ahead. Man, just look at the size of that crater. It's a wonder the entire planet didn't shatter when that hit."

Commander Volkov reached past him to transfer the images of the surface to the large screen. "I see what you mean. Look there, see that trench? Whatever hit them it must have been a glancing blow, akin to a billiard ball shot. It hit, bounced off, and spun them out to a deeper orbit of the star. Are we getting anything at all?"

The man had turned to a different screen. "Some metals, Commander, but nothing large, could be bits of a shattered hull, or maybe just rich ore deposits. Do you want to take a closer look at some of them?"

"No, stay on grid until we find something worth looking at."

They continued to scan as they flew a tight grid across the planet. As the lump of frozen rock slowly turned on its axis the light moved away from the damaged side of the planet on to a less disturbed area. Still nothing. Recovery One returned to a low orbit and parked for a sleep period.

Nine hours later she dropped low and resumed her search. Three hours after that they hit pay dirt. It was a ship, buried under tons of loose rock, dust and sand, but it was a ship, almost twice as big as Recovery One, and it looked to be intact. Recovery dropped down nearby, and her salvage crews spilled out. Two days later they reached an entry hatch.

The ship had been tossed upside down and buried.

* * * * *

The Crew of Explorer was ready as soon as Commander Drake stepped on board. "Three, are you ready on pilot?"

"Ready at pilot, Commander."

"Thirteen, is the crew ready?"

"Crew is ready, Commander. We also have three extra medical staff in case we find survivors."

"Take us out, Three."

The ship slipped easily out of the launch bay and shot toward the dark side of the frozen planet. She swept into a parking orbit above the place where they'd found Morthel and Antha. "It's a bit early by our standards but get some rest people. We'll be busy enough once the light reaches this side of the planet."

The ship was put on auto then everybody retired to the sleeping quarters. Eight hours later the alarm sounded. Amanda was already up and at the scanners. "Let's get to it, people. Sun's up. It's not a lot of light, but it's what we've got to work with.

"This mission is different from the last one. This time we're not concerned with tech, we're looking for bodies. We need to clear this entire area before Recovery One gets here. They're on salvage, we're on rescue.

"Antha, Morel."

"Right here, Commander Drake."

"Talk to me, ladies. What happened that day and where do I find others who got left behind?"

"It was terrifying," said Antha. "I was out at the community hall, preparing for a celebration. We had been working with new recruits who were preparing to move on the next planet. As I understand it, the planet where Captain Sorenson and the SUVI spent many years. Morthel stayed home to work on her journal.

"Suddenly we were all thrown to the ground, the buildings collapsing all around us. We scrambled outside to see a great wave of black storm hurtling toward us, the sky was burning. I fled home as fast as I could. Once inside we locked down the entryway and sealed the windows.

"The storm swept over the colony, throwing ships and buildings around, but our home survived, many didn't. Our communicators began to chatter, everyone was to gather and board a ship to leave. When we arrived at the departure point not enough ships were available, a lottery was issued, I was chosen to go, Morthel wasn't. I stayed with her and let another go in my place.

"We returned home, but the air was so cold, and it was hard to breathe. I remember shivering, choking, then nothing more until I awoke aboard the Reacher."

Amanda gently patted the tiny woman's shoulder. "Morthel?"

"That was it, Commander. I picked myself off the floor to rush out, looking for Antha, but found her hurrying towards me. We fled back inside and secured the home as best we could. After a night of terror, we were informed to gather for evacuation, but I wasn't allotted a seat and sweet Antha wouldn't go without me.

"We knew we were going to die, so we returned home and settled down for the end. She stopped breathing and I held her close, then woke up on the Reacher, terrified, and trying to understand Linsey's terrible accent."

Amanda smiled. "She admitted you had trouble with that. However, in her defense, it was Linsey and Eighteen's efforts that managed to bring Ship on side as well as help you understand that we mean you no harm."

"I know," smiled Morthel. "Linsey and her beloved Eighteen have become friends, more, they feel like family. Linsey still makes us help her practice our language. She says she wants to get it right."

"You asked for me to come on this mission, Commander. How may I serve?"

"Yes, Antha, you were active in the community. Of the people who got left behind, where would they go? Where would we locate them?"

"Commander, can we land, go outside where you found us? From there I should be able to recall where the houses are."

"All right, let's suit up. Pilot, set us down easy. Lilly, how many crates did you bring?"

"Eight, Commander. That's all we can carry."

"Then we're good to go."

As they stepped out of the ship everyone was wearing enviro suits. Morthel commented on how well hers fit. "Linsey had them made especially for you. She tried to find some on Ship, but that part of Ship was missing. Are they working all right for you?"

"Only one thumb on the glove is a bit awkward, but we'll manage. Antha, my most cherished, do you know if Ernel and Ovron got away?"

"I don't know. We can check their house first. It should be right over there." They all moved away in the direction Antha indicated. "It all looks so different, like an abandoned planet just newly discovered by explorers. Oh, Morthel, it ... so long ago ... I ..."

"Antha!" That snapped her out of it. "Focus, my beloved, find our friends now, sweet Antha."

"Of course. Forgive me, I just can't seem to encompass the magnitude of the time lost between that day and this one. This way."

They found one body intact, but the other had been crushed when a wall had collapsed sometime in the past. By the end of the day they had three more. They transported them directly to the medical bay aboard the Reacher. By nightfall the next day they'd found two more and buried several others that had been broken in the past.

"I'm sorry, Antha, I wish there were more we could do."

"No apologies, Commander. You saved us, returned us to life, took us from that planet of death where we were all left behind. Now you search for more, but time has been long, and the universe unkind to so many. We have found six possible, more than we had a right to expect. There will be no more to be found in this community, but there are two more to explore."

"We'll start at first light."

"Thank you, Commander. Now, with your permission I would withdraw to privacy."

"Antha ..."

"So much time lost, Commander Drake. How does the mind begin to grasp that the withered skeleton found was a living breathing friend mere days ago?"

Amanda sank into a seat and patted the one beside her. Antha sat down, not making eye contact. "Antha, we call that feeling you have, survivor guilt. You feel unworthy of life when so many others are denied it. We all, all us humans, have felt this, feel it now. Once there were billions of us, now barely a few thousand."

"You do understand. How do your people cope with this?"

"Everybody's different, we each cope in our own way. Mostly we try to form relationships, friendships with people we can talk to, feel safe to share our thoughts with."

"Compared to us there are so many of you. Will Morthel and I be able to make friends among your people, do you think?"

"I think you already have, Antha. Linsey and Eighteen would surely call themselves your friend, and me as well. I'm sure we'll be great friends. Ah, there comes Morthel and Mr. Sacumbtu. They're the last. Once we've all eaten, we'll retire for the night."

Antha hurried to help Morthel from her enviro suit and Amanda watched her with a sad smile. She'd have to keep a close eye on that poor girl. Amanda couldn't imagine falling asleep to wake up eons later, her people gone, and in the company of a strange species.

Two days later, as the salvage crews reached an entry port to the buried ship, the Explorer returned to the Reacher. In total they had found only eleven bodies they felt were viable, there had been dozens that were damaged or crushed. They delivered them to medical then returned to join Recovery One. They were ready if the salvage crews found more bodies on the downed ship.

Chapter 10

Busy Days

They'd been orbiting the frozen planet for over a week. Suvi-jean called a senior staff meeting and invited Miriam Holbrooke to sit in. "Are we all here?"

"All present, Captain."

"Thank you, Brandon. All right, let's get to it. Commander da Silva, report. How are all things salvage and recovery going?"

Linsey sat with her mouth working, but no sound coming out. Finally, she shook off the spell. "Captain, did you just promote me again?"

The captain just grinned at her. "Yes, I did. Linsey, when you and Eighteen were working alone, you were an ensign as befitted the task. I promoted you to Sub-Commander when the job grew to include all things alien. I'm happy to say you rose to the challenge and succeeded beyond expectation, but the job has grown again. I'm told you've excelled once more, so Commander, how about that report."

"Wow, thank you Captain. Right, report. Well, on the recovery of personnel I'm told we have fourteen possible bodies. I'm sure Commander Drake can give you better numbers.

"On the salvage side, Recovery One has gathered a wealth of metal and spare parts plus two intact ships, one another shuttle like Ship 87643, the other was an ore carrier for the mines. Both are possible to repair as far as I know.

"Captain, I'll admit I've left the recovery and salvage to the people better equipped to deal with that sort of thing. I've gone back to the office, pulled Morthel and Antha into my staff, and begun work on compiling as much information as I can of our target planet as well as on the empire they fled.

"We've also set ourselves up to assist any Earalith we may be able to revive."

Jeannie nodded as she absorbed all Linsey had told her. "Well done, Linsey. Carla, what's the word from Medical?"

"Well, Captain, we've had a few sprains and such from overeager salvage crews, but no real harm done. We were brought fourteen Earalith and have managed to revive three so far. Five of the bodies did not respond and were transferred to the morgue. I have hopes for the remaining six. Sorry, Captain, best I could do."

"Carla, I'm amaze you've been so successful. I'll admit that when I first ordered them thawed out I only hoped we would get a good look at them. What you've managed is nothing short of miraculous.

"Commander Drake, report."

"The Explorer checked and rechecked every building we could find, Captain. Most were damaged and most of the bodies we found were damaged as well. We buried those we found as best we could.

"On the home front, the colonists have elected Miriam to be their representative. She is here today to keep an eye on us."

"Well done, Commander. Tell me, how did our two Earalith do as crew members?"

"Quite well, actually. I'd like to offer them a permanent assignment to the Explorer if you'll agree."

"That's your ship, it's your decision to make, but I do approve. I like it. Commander Volkov?"

"Recovery One performed above expectation, Captain. The ship is sound and strong. I'm proud of my crew and how well they performed. We've filled the Reacher's cargo hold with scrap metal and spare parts for Earalithian ships, another small shuttle ship, and an ore hauler we can convert to a second salvage ship."

"A second salvage ship?"

"Yes, my first officer could be talked into commanding her, I mean him. Earalithian ships are operated by male identifying AIs."

"Your first officer?"

"Yes, I believe you're familiar with his credentials."

Jeannie chuckled as she leaned back and spoke again. "Engineering, report."

Moira Duncan's eyes were twinkling with excitement as she replied. "Ah, Captain, the good ship Recovery has brought us a wealth of strong metals, spare parts, and best of all, a complete engineering manual from entry level to a full command understanding of the ships and their working parts. It's been years since I've had such fun."

"Talk to me, Moira, what can we expect from all of this?"

"Improved engines to start. Give me two months and I expect we'll be able to triple our former best speed with half the energy expenditure. We've already managed to repair Ship 87643 and believe he's ready for a test flight. He says he's just waiting for Captain da Silva to board."

"Ship has been teasing me about that deception since he figured it out. So, he wants to take me for a ride, does he? Sure, I'm game if the Captain approves."

"How about it, Moira, is it safe for Linsey to play?"

"Everything checks out, Captain. The AI's fully accepted Linsey as the woman in command of all things Earalith, and he seems to be good with that. On the rest of it, well, all systems are functional and he's airtight for sure. Hell, I'll go myself."

"Don't want Linsey to get the first ride in an Earalith ship?"

"No, Jeannie, I don't. I want to do it, but the dang AI wants his captain."

"Let's both do it, Commander Duncan."

"Aye, that's a fair compromise, Linsey. You've got a deal."

"All right, let's get to the hard stuff now. Commander Singh, report."

"Captain Sorenson, did you just ... of course you did, thank you for the promotion. Yes, the report. All quiet aboard the Reacher, Captain."

Suvi-jean chuckled and grinned at the Security officer. "The best part of all that was Sheila did it without blinking. Doctor Reilly, how many people do you have in cryo chambers now?"

He sighed and looked at his hands. "Forty-one."

Jeannie grinned and leaned her elbows on the table. "I assume that takes care of my original list."

"Captain, I know those men deserve a fair trial, but under the circumstances I felt ..."

"Relax, Sheila. Tell me what made you move against this last group?"

"I did, Captain."

"Miriam?"

"Look, I saw that bunch jump you and promised that would never happen again. I made a few discrete enquiries, contacted Commander Singh, she enquired further, sent Jake White and his team in, and the result is we're free of another bunch of abusive violent troublemakers. As spokeswoman for the colonists, we have no issues with any of this."

"Nor do I," sighed the captain as she relaxed back in her chair. "All right then, are we finished with Frigid? Should we now return to our original target, or should we remain here for a while more?"

"I believe we should remain here for a good while yet, Captain."

"First Officer Hoffman?"

"Captain, we're reviving Earalith, refitting and perhaps even building more small ships of Earalith design, plus making modifications to the Reacher. Below us on the planet is more material we might need, we might learn of a more likely planet, ..."

"Moira put you up to this didn't she?"

The chief Engineer gave a great laugh. "I confess we did chat a bit about the possibilities."

"In truth, I was leaning in that direction as well. However, before we make that decision I'd like to hear from the colonists. Miriam?"

"Actually, I'm with these folks, Captain. We went charging in on Elysium, and we damn near got wiped out. I'd like us to learn all we can here, then go on to the next likely planet, explore it thoroughly, make sure it's relatively safe, before trying to colonize it. We're with you on this one. Nobody on this ship is in a hurry to go groundside again. Next time we want to be sure.

* * * * *

While the captain and senior staff were feeling good about all that had been accomplished, things were a bit more tense in Medical. <Antha, how could you do this to me?>

<Lady Ernel, I don't understand. Lady, I did nothing to you, of what do you speak?>

<Why am I here in this strange place? Where is Ovron?>

<Alas, Ovron could not be revived. A wall had fallen.>

<What does that mean? Tell me.>

Morthel stepped in, put her arm around Antha protectively. <When we were asked to find others who might be recalled from a frozen death, Antha immediately sought out your house. Sometime in the past, a wall had fallen. Ovron's shattered body lay beneath it. Ernel, there was nothing to be done.>

Ernel was weeping now. <How am I supposed to go on without him? What will these aliens do with us? Will we be returned to the empire? Oh sweet spirits, Ovron ... What is to become of me now?>

<We don't know for certain, but Linsey assures us we will not be harmed. These people have worked hard to revive as many of our people as possible. We are now eleven. I've spoken to Linsey about this, and she has promised to speak with the captain on our behalf. Also, we've been ordered to report to Explorer after next sleep cycle. We're going out again to check for more people. Commander Drake doesn't want to miss a single Earalith who could be revived.>

<Yes, but ...> She got no further as the captain walked in accompanied by Commander Drake, Linsey, and Eighteen.

Morthel hopped off her chair and saluted the captain who laughed with delight. "Thank you, Morthel, that was perfect. Linsey."

"Working, Captain." She was passing out translation tablets. <When you speak this will translate for the captain. When she speaks, it will do the same for you. In this way all will understand one another.>

"Greetings, people of Earalith. I'm Captain Sorenson of the spaceship Reacher. I'm certain you're confused, unsettled, and have many questions. I came to speak with you here rather than confuse the issue further by having you moved all over the ship at this time of awakening.

"I'm sure you're wondering what will happen to you in the days to come. We have several options available to us, but ultimately your fate will lie in your own hands."

The man who'd been asking questions before spoke up, bowing his head deferentially. "May I ask what some of those options are?"

"Look up to my eyes, my friend. There is no need to fear me. Now, some of your options; we hope you will all consider joining with us, become part of our group as we search space for a new home.

"Commander Drake has offered Morthel and Antha a post on Explorer, Commander da Silva has offered them a post on her staff as well. We have also managed to salvage and repair a small ship of Earalithian design. If you so choose we will supply it as best we can, and let you go your own way with our blessing.

"Each of you will be able to choose your own destiny even as we SUVI did. Allow me to explain. The human species tried to colonize a planet in the next system. I believe your own people did also. On that planet we encountered a deadly virus that nearly wiped us out. Nineteen of us managed to survive but were enslaved by the other colonists.

"When we arrived on the Reacher, we SUVI were given these same options. We chose to remain aboard the Reacher and have managed to fit in, to find our place. It could be the same for you.

"Rest and grow strong again. There's no hurry to make any decisions right now. When our Chief Medical Officer, Commander

Marks, feels you're ready, Linsey will help you find quarters where you will be more comfortable.

"So, are there any more questions?"

"Captain, sweet Antha and I have discussed our future here aboard the Reacher. I fear Antha did not enjoy her time in an enviro suit. She would prefer to remain here to work with Commander da Silva.

"I would like that as well, but I did quite enjoy working with Commander Drake aboard the Explorer. As I understand this, if I accept the post to Explorer, I will still be able to work with Commander da Silva while the Explorer is aboard the Reacher."

"That's how it works all right," smiled Amanda. "Happy to have you aboard, Morthel. You'll be my official consultant about all things Earalith. You'll have to work closely with Linsey's department."

"All right, people, we'll let you rest now. Sleep well." With that Suvi-jean took Amanda's hand and led her out of the medical bay.

They didn't get far when they met Olga Volkov and Sheila Singh coming towards them. "Captain, can you spare us a few minutes?"

"Is it too late to run away?"

Olga grinned. "Oh, it's way too late for that."

"Why do I suspect you two are going to make a lot of work for me?"

"Why Suvi-jean, I'm shocked you would even think such a thing."

"Sheila Singh, by the grin on your face I can tell you're going to get me back for that Jonah Thornton escapade. All right, let's head to the briefing room. I refuse to let you embarrass me in the corridors."

As they turned their steps toward the bridge, Commander Volkov spoke again. "Captain, perhaps a full staff meeting would be in order."

"First you fill me in, then we'll let the others in on it. Here we are, ladies. Go ahead, hit me with it."

Olga Volkov sighed and began. "Jeannie, of all your senior staff, I'm the oldest. I was actually considering retirement when you rode that damned monster onto the ship. Since then my job has gotten busier.

Brandon is a lot younger than me, and he's a natural details guy, perfect for the job."

"Ah-huh, but you'll want to stay in command of Recovery, am I right?"

Olga grinned at that. "Look at it as semi-retirement."

"Okay, Sheila, what's your story?"

"I'm only a few years from retirement, but I was thinking of going early."

"Why?"

"Well, it's complicated."

Amanda grinned with delight. "Let me, Captain. I think this is one of those places where I can be of help." Jeannie nodded so she went on, addressing Sheila. "Let me guess. You enjoyed your role as the sexy girlfriend when you guys were trying to find the virus, so did the security guy."

"Markus."

"Markus. So, with a new romance under way, you want more time off, plus, with him reporting to you as his supervisor, it could get awkward, right?"

"Yeah, that's pretty much it."

"And, as a woman who likes to have things working smoothly, you already have a plan."

"Yes, I retire, and Jake White gets the top job."

The captain sighed and leaned her elbows on the table, her eyes glowing amber. "Ladies, I'm not happy about this, not at the present time with all that's going on. However, I won't gainsay you, but I would like to call in the rest of the senior staff, get their take on this."

They both nodded as she reached for her comm. "This is the captain, all senior staff to the bridge, repeat, all senior staff to the bridge. Ensign Jake White to the bridge."

Once they all assembled, Jeannie laid it out for them. Brandon Hoffman turned to Olga Volkov. "So, you want to saddle me with the tough job and go play, is that it?"

"In a nutshell, Brandon. Look, we both know Frank Baris gave me the job because I was the senior captain when we blended the crews, you were always a better choice and you know it."

He didn't respond until the captain prompted him. "Brandon?"

"Yeah, can't deny I always wanted the job. Sheila is a better security officer. I always look after the details and make her do the investigative stuff."

"Maybe, but Jake's way better at it than I am. He'll make a fine Chief of Security."

"Captain, may I speak to this?"

"Sure Jake, what have we missed?"

"A bunch of stuff," he grinned. "First, Commander Singh loves her job."

"Oh yeah? What makes you think I love that job?"

"Commander, you have a new love interest, yet you're always at work early, and you leave late, even when we tell you to go home, there's nothing important to do. So, you love the job, but Markus reports to you, that's an issue for you, maybe for him, but you retiring isn't the best solution here."

"Really, so enlighten us, why isn't it?"

"Commander Singh, you know damn well that as an ensign I can go places, learn things, that would be impossible for me as Chief of Security."

"Still watching my back, big brother?"

"Yes, Captain, now and always. There's still a couple of characters I want to keep an eye on. So, here's my solution to the problem. Explorer is short one security guy because my captain won't leave the Reacher, so neither will I. Transfer Marcus to Explorer, put him under Commander

Drake's command and thereby remove the problem for Commander Singh."

"Damn you're good," grinned the Captain. "Thank you for that stellar solution, Sub-Commander White."

Jake gave her a wide grin at that. "Thank you for the promotion, Captain, but can we hold that back for a while, just until I finish a little project I'm working on?"

"All right, Jake. Let me know when you're ready and the promotion will go on the books. Sheila does this solution work for you?"

"It does, Captain, but it depends on Commander Drake. Explorer is her ship."

"I can take him on Recovery if it makes things easier. I don't have any Security people right now."

"I have no problem at all, Captain, but Commander Volkov is right. Our ships are small, minimal crews, one Security man each should be enough."

"All right, Mandy, that makes sense. So, does this work for everybody?" There were nods of agreement all round. "Any further discussion?" There was none. "Then so be it. Brandon, I now confirm you as First Officer, Sheila, you're the official Chief of Security, and Jake, you're the secret Sub-Commander. As such you can inform Marcus of his transfer.

"Commander Volkov, your request for retirement is accepted, however, I still need you in command of Recovery One. Who knows what trouble that first officer of yours would get into if I gave him free reign."

"I'll tell him you said that."

"Don't you dare," laughed Jeannie. "Is there anything else?"

"I'd like to confirm Jake as my second in command, Captain. We work well as a team."

"Confirmed. Anything more?"

"Actually, I'd like to semi-retire to have more time with my lover too," grinned Amanda.

"Mandy?"

"From Social engagement, Darin is practically running the show anyway."

"I see. Very well, I relieve you of that command and give you another job. Commander Drake, you are now the Captain's Aide. You will report directly to me when not on the Explorer. Your first task is to go promote somebody to the Social Engagement position, give him the appropriate boost in rank as well. He will report directly to you.

"Are we done yet, or are the rest of you planning to abandon me? Moira, tell me you're not thinking about retiring."

"Me? Oh hell no. I've sat around, bored to tears for twenty years, and now we suddenly have new metals, exciting advancements in engineering, and more. I'm just getting started."

"Good news indeed. Now I want to add a little something to the mix here. All personnel assigned to the smaller ships will have no further duties aboard the Reacher unless they so desire. When said ships are parked the crew will spend their time training, studying, and otherwise doing whatever is needed to make them better as a smaller crew.

"All right, people, let's get back to work."

Chapter 11

Foreboding

Five people sat chatting easily, enjoying their break. They were sitting amid a mass of salvaged metals and parts. Suddenly one man's head came up, sensing danger. "Thirteen?"

"Hisst!" He was on his feet, eyes searching everywhere, every instinct reaching out, seeking, the sense of the danger urging him to flee. Suddenly he leaped away, diving to the deck then rolling back to his feet, a bladed weapon in his hand.

He blushed deeply and relaxed his stance at the sound of the woman's laughter. A note written on a sticky tab was attached to his chest, yet he hadn't actually seen her or felt the contact. "Got you!"

"Come out, SUVI 5, you're still the best hunter."

"You're getting slack." She was smiling with delight as she emerged from a pile of alien parts, straightening her uniform.

That remark caught his attention, and he straightened up. "So, you've felt it too?"

"I have, Thirteen. It's faint, but I wanted to check with you anyway. Have you taken a closer look?"

"No, Captain, but I've been meaning to. Have you asked Eighteen?"

"Not yet, but this is more your sort of thing than hers. Where would you be most comfortable?"

Thirteen paused for only an instant. "Explorer."

"Let's go." They walked away leaving the others to wonder what had just happened. One thing was clear, the captain was good enough to sneak up on Thirteen and fast enough to tag him and survive. She was clearly a dangerous woman.

They arrived to find the ship empty. "I'll watch, you take a look." Thirteen nodded and settled into a seat while Suvi-jean stepped outside and closed the hatch. It was a long wait before he opened it again.

His eyes were glowing amber when he opened the hatch and, with a jerk of his head, invited her to join him. She entered then locked the hatch behind her. "Well?"

"It's a jumble, Five, hard to make sense of. The danger is twofold, both to do with the Earalith, yet separated in time. Our people, the ones we've revived aren't directly involved. One is an event of sudden nature, the other a result of passed time.

"I first saw an explosion of some sort. I have no idea of the cause, or where it originates. However, I believe it to be on the planet, not the ship. The second event is still in the future and may or may not be of major significance. It mostly rests on the first event. If that goes badly then the second will be worse. If we can contain the first, it may prevent the second from have any lasting effect."

The captain sat mulling that over for a while. Thirteen made no attempt to disturb her thoughts. Finally she raised her head. "Recommendations?"

"Proceed with caution, also I'd like to put Earalithian metal shields on the Explorer as well as Recovery One."

"Agreed. I'll set that in motion. Thirteen ..."

"I'll watch her back, Five, and I'll protect her with my life. After all, she's starting to use her brain. You'll need her in the future."

"I need her now, Thirteen. I need her now."

"Captain, may I ask ...?"

"Yes, I train every day, just as you taught me."

"Then I need to work harder. From where I sat you should never have reached me unseen. Perhaps all SUVI should begin a regimen of training their special talents."

"I get the sense that's a good idea, Thirteen. Put the word out, but quietly. Human/ SUVI relations are good right now, no point scaring the more paranoid among them."

"Quietly, as you say, Captain Sorenson." She grinned and gave his arm a friendly squeeze as she popped open the hatch and strode away.

Shaking his head slowly, he watched her go. "How in hell did she get that close to me before I sensed her. Oh yeah, I truly do need to increase my training. That's not going to happen again."

Jeannie was just reaching for her comm to inform Engineering of the need for Earalithian shields when the Reacher rocked slightly. "Captain to the bridge, repeat, Captain to the bridge. Emergency!"

The bridge was a busy place as Jeannie came through the door at a run. Commander Jones was standing before the view screen, a stream of orders being issued as he worked the sensors himself. "Captain."

"As you were, Emmet. Get things under control, I'll wait."

A few moments later reports began to pour in. "Engineering reporting. Hull breached, minor damage, breach sealed, no major systems affected, full repairs under way."

"Understood, Engineering."

"Security reporting. A few minor panics, nothing serious, all contained."

"Understood, Security."

"Medical reporting. A few minor injuries, nothing more from Reacher. Preparing for incoming injured from Recovery."

"Understood Medical." Emmet Jones relaxed his shoulders and turned to the captain.

"Emmet, what happened?"

"Unknown, Captain. Something hit us a glancing blow, but Recovery didn't fare so well. She's free floating and we can't raise her."

"You have the bridge." Jeannie turned and ran toward the launch bay. "This is the captain, all Explorer crew to the ship on the double. Repeat, Explorer Crew to the ship on the double."

Most of them were there when she arrived. Fortunately, Amanda had been there with them taking inventory of ship's supplies. "Three, warm up the engines. Jake lock her up and strap in."

"Destination Captain?"

"Recovery is in trouble; we're going after her. We're a lot more maneuverable than Reacher."

"Understood. Doors opening, we're clear to launch, and we're out in space."

Jeannie had taken the co-pilot's seat and was scanning the area. Amanda leaned over her shoulder. "Three, come about eighty degrees, five degrees down plane. Good, there's Recovery, drifting away. Looks like they've managed to right her, but that's all."

A voice sounded over the comms, crackling and fading in and out. A moment later it cleared up. "This is Recovery One calling Reacher. Do you copy, Reacher? Come on, dammit, work. Hold that tighter there. This is Recovery One calling Reacher, do you copy, Reacher?"

That voice was answered by the voice of Commander Drake. "Recovery One, this is Explorer on rendezvous course. Have you got life support?"

"We're a little beat up over here, Amanda. Olga is out cold and so is our engineer. Chance Morita and I have managed to get the damn comms working, and we've stabilized her a bit, but the main engine is offline. Our medic is a busy boy, but on the whole, we're still in one piece.

"I guess we don't have enough juice in this damned comm to reach the main ship. Can you contact them for us and let Jeannie know I'm still kicking?"

"I'm right here, Grandfather. It's good to hear your voice. Hang on now, we'll hook on and tow you back to the Reacher."

"Good news indeed."

"Grandfather, can you tell me what happened?"

"We were hovering about ten meters above the surface, using the main laser drill to cut away some rock. The drill must have hit a gas pocket and ignited it. The explosion threw us out into space, we bounced off the side of Reacher then spun away. Jeannie, we had three men on the surface. They're in enviro suits, but I have no idea how they fared."

"I'll contact the Reacher and let them know about the men on the surface. Okay, we're here, hooking on."

The two ships bumped gently then the Explorer extended an air seal around the Recovery's main hatch. A few moments later Explorer's new medic and her engineer were aboard Recovery. While the crews worked Jeannie turned to Amanda with a look of contrition. "Commander Drake, I owe you a huge apology."

"Jeannie?"

"I panicked, Mandy. Grandfather's ship was in trouble, and I raced down here and tried to take over. You remained calm, took command of your ship, and efficiently got things under control. My place was on the bridge of the Reacher, not trying to take over your ship."

"Jeannie, Explorer is your ship, you designed her, built her, and commanded her. She's your ship."

"Was my ship, Mandy, but no longer. You know this ship, this crew, and they respond to you, work as an efficient team for you. You, not me. The Reacher is my ship now. Explorer is your command. I'll just sit here and be quiet while you deal with the current situation."

"Jeannie ..."

"Five is right, Commander Drake. Things have evolved, situations have changed, stay focused on the now."

"Thirteen."

"Shut up?"

"Suit up and take a look at Recovery's hull, make sure we don't tear her apart when we tighten the lines."

"Ma'am."

Thirteen was grinning as he turned away and went to get into his enviro suit. "That'll hold him for a while. Mr. Sacumbtu?"

"Ready with the grapples, Commander."

"Hold back until Thirteen gives the okay."

"Understood."

Jeannie was smiling at Amanda. "What?"

"You, my bewitchingly beautiful companion. You ever so gently took back control of your ship and crew, and things have smoothed right out, Recovery is being recovered, her crew administered to, and I'm in awe of you. I should make you captain."

A slow grin of mischief spread across Amanda's face. "Forget that, Suvi-jean, I know what you're up to. You're not making me captain of the Reacher so you can steal my ship and go play. Your grandfather may have pulled that one on you, but you're not doing it to me."

Suvi-jean laughed heartily at that. "Darn, it was worth a try. Seriously, Mandy, I'm so proud of you, but I'm just in the way here. Transport me back onto the Reacher where I can do something useful." She walked back to stand on the transport pad. Amanda kissed her cheek then threw the switch. The captain reappeared on the Reacher in a flash of light.

She strode onto the bridge, smiling. "Report, Mr. Jones."

"Recovery is on her way home towed by the Explorer, Captain. We've retrieved the three men from the surface of Frigid. One dead, one injured, and one relatively intact, but badly shaken."

"Well done, Emmet. I'll ask Brandon to arrange the funeral service for the man who perished." Emmet nodded.

"You have the bridge." Suvi-Jean left the bridge, her heart heavy with the loss of another crew member. She found her first officer at his desk.

"We lost a man today."

"I heard," said Brandon. "Bad news travels fast on the Reacher. I'll make the necessary arrangements Captain."

"Thank you Brandon."

She left her first officer and headed down to meet the returning ships. She found Moira Duncan there with a full crew. "Moira."

"Captain?"

"I was on my way to talk to you when the excitement started."

"Oh?"

"I was thinking both Explorer and Recovery could use some shields made of Earalithian metals."

Moira chuckled at that. "I was on my way to find you to recommend that very thing. It'll take us a while to patch up Recovery and get the shields in place."

"Do it, Moira. I'll keep Amanda and her crew searching for possible survivors, but I'll warn them off trying to salvage anything. You beef up Recovery. I want her tough as a battleship before she goes back to work. Once she's ready for service, pull Explorer in for the same refit. I just wish I could add better shields to the Reacher."

"Aye, well, I've been a bit busy, but I've been working on something like that."

"Moira?"

"Energy shields. I've learned a bunch from reading Earalithian manuals, texts, and such, but I'd like to get your mother's input on it."

"My mother?"

"That genetic memory of yours is an amazing tool, Jeannie. If you can spare a bit of time we could put our heads together and I think we could make it work."

"All right, Moira, once we get things under control here, we'll get together and see what we can come up with. It'll probably have to wait until we're interstellar again, but ..."

The voice over the loudspeaker interrupted her. "Explorer and Recovery returning. Clear the docking area, repeat, ships returning. Clear the docking area."

The docking was a bit rough, but they got the wounded Recovery back inside with Explorer and closed the main doors. As the crew was being taken off the damaged ship and checked out, the first officer of Recovery One was seized in a bear hug by the captain of the Reacher. "Jeannie, I'm all right. Put me down, girl. It's unseemly for a captain to be hugging a first officer in public."

She matched his grin as she gently released him. "Report, Grandfather."

"Aye, Captain. When the explosion tossed us away we'd have been fine, but we bounced off the Reacher. That probably didn't feel like much here, but it was pretty intense for us. Olga tried to shield me and took a head injury. Several others got knocked around a bit, and we took damage to our comms, engine control, and more.

"Chance Morita managed to patch together something that allowed us to regain life support and stabilize the ship. We were working on getting the engines back online when you came running to the rescue."

"Actually, it was Mandy who organized the rescue. To my great embarrassment, I wasn't very captain like, and she had to take over for me. You'd be proud of her, Grandfather, she has that crew of hers operating at peak efficiency. While I was trying to think of what to do next she and her crew rescued you. I transported back to the Reacher to get out of the way and let them work."

"So, you've lost your ship?" he grinned.

"No, Grandfather, the Reacher is my ship. I know that now, and I also know the Explorer is in good hands. Come on, let's go see if Carla has your captain patched up yet."

Amanda joined them as they entered the medical bay. A freshly bandaged Olga Volkov was waiting for them. She started to rise, but Carla patted her shoulder to sit her back down. "Oh no you don't, you stay right there. I want to keep an eye on you for a couple of days."

"All right, Carla," sighed Olga as she relaxed back. "How are you doing, Frank? Are you functional?"

"I am, Captain Volkov. Orders?"

"Stop your damn grinning, go see to the crew, and then wheedle Moira into fixing our ship."

"It'll just get blown up again," muttered a soft voice behind them. They all turned to see a male Earalithian standing there.

"Who are you? What do you mean by that?"

"You are Captain Sorenson, the one we owe our lives to, are you not? Captain Sorenson, I am Dorind. I was the engineer of an ore hauler on the planet you call Frigid. I know it is now, but it was a paradise when we found it.

"Yes, the explosion. There are pockets of explosive gasses all over the planet, or at least there were. If you hit one with a laser drill it will explode. The trick is to find them first."

"Tell me, Dorind, do you know how to find them?"

"I do. I apologize for speaking out of turn, Captain. I was just returning from ship 87643, learning your language, when I heard people talking about the explosion. I knew instantly what had happened. You need a special sensor to detect the pockets of gas."

"Dorind, you're just the man we need. As you know, we want the Earalith to feel at home here, to join the crew of the Reacher, to be part of our people. Will you do it? Will you join with us?"

"In truth, Captain, I had thought to ask for the small ship and to go my own way, for I couldn't see how I might fit in here, be of use to the collective peoples. However, I believe I do have skills and knowledge that will be useful. I will stay if you wish."

"I do wish, friend Dorind. Are you ready to go to work? I'm quite sure the chief engineer would love to have you on her crew."

At his nod she chuckled and reached for her comm. "Captain to Chief Engineer Duncan."

"Here, Captain."

"Moira, I have a man here who wants to work with you."

"Oh? What's his claim to fame?"

"He's an Earalithian Engineer with extensive experience. Got a spot on your crew for him?"

"Oh, you know I do. How soon can I have him?"

"Dorind says he's ready to go to work. Send somebody to the infirmary to get him."

"I'll come myself. Be right there." The excitement was clear in her voice.

"She'll be here in a minute, Dorind. Prepare yourself, she'll want to pick your brain for every ounce of knowledge you have."

"I too will want to learn all I can of your systems. Perhaps between us we will be able to improve on both."

Jeannie chuckled at that. "You two will get along just fine."

Later that day Jeannie relaxed back in the cuddling chair. Amanda settled in with her for a cuddle and a soft kiss for her hair. "I'm glad I don't have to be the super captain here in our quarters."

"What is it, sweetheart? Something's been bugging you for days."

"I sense grave danger closing in on us, Mandy. I checked in with Thirteen, but he couldn't pinpoint it either. I thought the explosion, and the results of that were it, but it wasn't. If that had been the danger, we'd be past it now, but I only feel it growing stronger."

"Any idea what it is?"

"None, nor does Thirteen, but it's got him on edge too."

"Yeah, I noticed that earlier today. Have you checked with Eighteen?"

"Not yet, it's on my list for tomorrow, provided nothing else goes wrong in the meantime."

"Aw, my poor Suvi-jean, she's all stressed out. How about I hug you until the stress melts away?"

"That would be really nice, Mandy, and there's something else you could do to speed up the process."

Amanda grinned with delight as she replied. "Oh? What might that be?"

"You could make me explode into stardust, my exquisite woman, launch me into blissful oblivion then wait and reassemble me without the stressful parts."

"Really? And how do you suggest I do that?"

"It starts with a kiss."

"Mmm, and then what happens?"

"I have no idea at all, sweet woman. Your magical kiss makes me forget everything, even my own name. All I know is, you kiss me, I float away on the sweetness of it, somewhere out there I explode and get put back together in a happier state. I'm afraid that, after the kiss, you'll have to experiment, for I have no idea what to do from there."

"I see." Amanda smiled with delight and licked her lips. "One big happy experiment coming right up." She pulled Jeannie closer for the kiss. "I so love experimenting." Jeannie groaned with delight as their lips met. Much later she drifted off to sleep, a smile of sweet contentment on her face.

Next morning, Jeannie strode into Linsey's office to see her watching Eighteen nervously. The SUVI woman was seated cross legged on the floor, her eyes closed, drawing deep regular breaths. Without opening her eyes or moving in any way, she spoke. "Good morning, Five. You are disturbed too?"

"I am, Eighteen. What can you tell me?"

"Oraks."

"Oraks?"

"I get a strong sense of Oraks. The doctor kept that container of virus on the ship, didn't he?"

"He did. He assures me it is perfectly safe. Is it not?"

"As long as it remained undisturbed, yes, but the container suffered injury when the two ships collided." Eighteen sighed and opened her eyes, they were glowing amber. "Dare I ask what is going on?"

Suvi-jean sighed and sank into a chair. "Strictest confidence, ladies. Dr. Reilly married long ago, but his wife became deathly ill. He put her into cryo sleep until he could devise a cure for her. She's still asleep and on this ship. He hopes the virus can defeat her disease, and the berries we brought to him can defeat the virus."

"You allowed this?"

"We were still trying to keep my promotion to captain secret when we acquired it. I dared not gainsay him in front of so many witnesses and he knew it."

"And afterwards?"

"We are SUVI, Eighteen, unique in all the worlds, and there are only eighteen of us still alive. I confess, I wondered if he might succeed, if we could become more, grow, and exist alongside the humans, part of a greater whole."

Eighteen nodded slowly, absorbing the idea. It was Linsey who spoke first. "Captain, are there steps we can take to make sure this woman gets a chance at life, and still protect the rest of the ship from the virus?"

"Now that I know what we're facing, I believe there are, Linsey. We'll need to seal off the area where he plans to wake her, make sure that only full SUVI are in attendance. That way, she can't infect anyone else if she goes wild. We're the only ones who are immune.

"The problem will be to make certain the damned virus is contained. That will mean keeping her in isolation until the virus has been rendered inert in her system, and also make certain it doesn't get loose in any other manner.

"I'll go see what I can do about this right now. Eighteen, you quietly connect with the other SUVI and have them stay alert, tell them why but don't let it get out to the general population. We don't want to start a panic."

With that she left the office and headed for the infirmary.

Chapter 12

SUVI 20

As the captain stepped into the infirmary, Carla saw her and approached. "Suvi-jean, what's wrong?"

"My instincts are going crazy, the same for Eighteen. Where is Eamon?"

"In his lab, right through there."

"Carla, when I close that door behind me, seal it and isolate the lab until I personally tell you otherwise."

"Jeannie?"

"Eighteen believes the container that houses the virus was damaged when the ships collided. Seal us off and prepare for an epidemic."

Carla had gone pale. She swallowed hard then nodded. "Okay, Jeannie, but we'll have to keep this quiet until we're sure, otherwise there'll be widespread panic aboard the ship."

"Yes, keep it quiet, but prepare. Did Eamon ever develop an antivirus?"

"I don't know. I don't."

"Do you have access to all his research?"

"Yes, all of it. All right, you do whatever you have to, I'll handle this end."

"See, I knew you were the right one for the top job."

"I hope you're right about that."

"I am. Lock me in now."

With that Jeannie stepped through the door to the research lab and closed it behind her. She heard the hiss of the air locks and a soft voice that disappeared almost as soon as it spoke. "Alert, biohazard, alert bio …"

Even as the warning was silenced Dr. Eamon Reilly spun towards the door. He was wearing a biohazard suit, but it had a syringe hanging loosely from where it had penetrated the material. On a cryo bed with the lid raised lay a woman who groaned in pain. Eamon's eyes were wide and frightened. He faced his captain even as the woman on the bed tried to sit up. "Jeannie?"

"Eamon, what happened?"

"Jeannie, I ... I'm so sorry, I ..."

The captain's eyes glowed amber as she took him by the shoulders. "Focus, tell me what happened." Her voice sounded strange, hollow, and yet, somehow utterly compelling.

"I was preparing the syringe. Tara was still asleep, but I wanted to give her the virus before she was fully awake. I pulled the container out of cold storage and started warming it up. Just as I filled the syringe the ship lurched, and the container was damaged. I got it back into the storage unit, and I waited as long as I dared, but Tara was waking up.

"I tried to hurry the process today, and managed to give her the shot, but she lashed out and I got stuck by the needle. I believe I'm infected."

"Have you the antidote?"

"I made enough for Tara, but that's all."

"Are there more berries?"

"No, I used them all. Jeannie ..."

"Tend to Tara now." She gently pushed him in the direction of the waking woman.

He turned toward the woman on the bed. "Tara, it's okay, it's all okay. Just relax back, everything will be fine."

"Eamon, is that you? What's going on? Why are you in a bio suit and that woman isn't?"

"It's all right, sweetheart. Trust me, it's all right. I just have to give you a shot now then I'll explain everything."

"I feel so strange, so hot ..."

"You'll be fine in no time, I promise. Jeannie, pass me that syringe."

"This one? This is the antidote?"

"Yes, I have to give it to her before the virus starts rewriting her DNA."

He held out his hand for the syringe, but never took his eyes off Tara. That was his mistake. Jeannie popped the cover off the needle then jabbed it into his arm. Eamon yelped and tried to jerk away, but she held him fast and gave him the shot. "Ow, what the hell are you doing? Tara needs that shot. God dammit, you've killed her."

He lunged at her, but Jeannie grabbed him and threw him to the floor. She knelt on his back to keep him still as she reached for her comm unit. "Captain to Eighteen. Please come to the infirmary and bring some of those resources we were speaking about earlier."

"On our way, Captain."

"Captain Sorenson to Commander Drake."

"Amanda here. What's up?"

"Bring your botanist and meet me in the infirmary. Captain out."

She stood and hauled Eamon to his feet. "You can get that bio suit off; it can't help you now. If your anti-virus is effective, you'll be fine, if not you may very well have killed every human on this ship."

He stood glaring at her. "That shot was for Tara, it was her only hope."

"And you were willing to risk every human still alive in the universe to give her that one chance. You'd risk your entire species on that one slim chance."

"You'd do the same if it was Amanda lying there."

"No, I wouldn't. You keep forgetting, I'm not human, I'm SUVI. No SUVI would take that risk."

"Gods I hurt. What's going on? Who are you people? What have you done to me? Walter why are you here and where is Eamon?"

Jeannie turned to her and sat on the edge of the bed. "You are Tara, I'm Suvi-jean, Captain of the Reacher."

"The Reacher? Eamon was assigned to the Far Star. I don't understand, what's going on?"

"I know. Just relax against me now and I'll explain everything." For some reason Tara felt comforted by this woman. She leaned against her and sighed.

"Why do I hurt so bad?"

"It's the virus. Listen now and I'll tell you a story. Over thirty years ago a brilliant young doctor loved his wife more than life itself. Sadly, the woman became deathly ill, and he put her into cryo sleep until the day when he could find a cure for her."

"He put me in cryo? I told him not to do that, I ..."

"I know, I know. He doesn't follow orders very well, does he? Anyway, on with my story. Our heroic doctor smuggled his lover onto his ship before it set out into the void to drop off a load of colonists. When the ships returned to Earth, they found the planet had been destroyed, unable to sustain any form of life. The captains of the five ships blended the crews to man a single ship, the Reacher, and set out to make a colony of their own.

"Many years passed, and no suitable planet was found. Eventually the Reacher returned to where she'd left her colonists in hopes to join them. Alas, that was not to be. That colony had been decimated by a virus that rewrites the DNA of a human, changing them forever into something very different from a human.

"I'm one such person, a SUVI, survivor of unknown viral infection. Now, our good doctor acquired some of that deadly virus and infected you with it."

"He did what???"

"Easy girl, easy. He hopes the virus will defeat the disease that threatens your life. Now, this is the part where it gets hard. You see, Eamon had an antidote for you. If all had worked according to plan, the antidote would have neutralized the virus as soon as it defeated the disease. The problem is, there was only one antidote, but unfortunately, as he was administering the virus to you, he infected himself.

"Tara, that man standing there is your husband, thirty years older. Eamon Reilly is a precious resource to this ship, to your entire species. We believe the Reacher contains every human left alive in the universe, and Eamon's medical expertise is invaluable to us. I gave him the antidote against his wishes, that's why he's so angry with me right now."

"All right, if all you say is true, you did the right thing, but what will happen to me now? Will I finally die? Will that stop the pain at last?"

"Quite possibly. The odds are against you, but some do survive. I'm living proof that it can be done. Here's what will happen now. Soon the pain in your body should stop, but your mind will grow fuzzy. Over the next few days you will battle the fever, and the pain, as they come and go in waves, your ability to focus will fade in and out as well. During this process the virus will rewrite your DNA, changing you into something else, a person like me.

"Only about ten per cent of those infected survive the fevers, and barely ten per cent of the survivors are able to clear their mind to become functional again. If you make it through the fevers you will face powerful urges to escape, to join with others like yourself, your new self.

"There are more like me on this ship, and I've sent for some of them. We'll stay with you so that should ease that madness somewhat, for we're already like you.

"Tara, I'm extremely intuitive, a gift from the virus. I have a sense you will make it through, that you will become an invaluable member of our people."

Tara was twisting and squirming, trying to get more comfortable. "You survived this agony?"

"Yes. My original designation was SUVI 5, the fifth survivor." Just then her comms pinged. "Jeannie here."

"It's Carla. Eighteen and friends have arrived, I'm sending them through the airlock." There was a hiss then the door unsealed, and three people entered, Eighteen, Four, and Nineteen."

"People, this is Tara, who will soon become SUVI 20."

"A pleasure to meet you, Tara. I'm Four," smiled the older woman. "This little gal is Eighteen, and our quiet friend there is Nineteen. "We're here to help you through the change."

"The change? You mean you're my nurses?"

"No, girl, we're your new family, your new herd, your people. Five, you go back to work, the ship needs her captain. We'll take care of Tara for you."

Jeannie nodded and gently passed Tara into Eighteen's arms. She stood and faced Eamon. "How are you feeling? Any pain in your joints?"

"No."

"Think fast, your grandmother's sister's name?"

He didn't hesitate. "Aunt Elsie. Why did you ask that?"

"Because if you were still infected you'd have no idea. Okay, no joint pain, clear head, you're good to go. Come on."

"No, I can't, I need to be here to monitor Tara. I ..."

"And you will be, but first we need to have a chat. Come on, don't make me drag you out of here."

With a deep sigh he shed the last of the bio suit and followed her out through the airlock. They emerged to find Carla, Amanda, and Lilly Peters waiting for them. "Carla, can I borrow your office for a few minutes?"

"Sure."

"Come on, people, we need to talk. You too, Carla." They trooped into the office behind her. "Everyone relax, sit. Eamon, are you all right?"

"Yes, I'm fine."

"Look, I know you're angry with me. The big problem here is you're just too damned human."

"So that's a bad thing?"

"In your case right now, yes. Eamon, I had to give you the antidote. We couldn't afford to lose you, you're too important to the continued survival of the human race. Now, having said that, we'll do everything in our power to help Tara make it through."

He relaxed his shoulders at last. "Jeannie, I'm begging you, put your best people on this, please."

"I will, Eamon. We'll send our best medic in to watch over her, but you'll have to be careful."

"What???"

"You're immune now, Carla's not, nor is any other of the medical staff, besides you're our best and I want our best caring for her. However, you have to understand, there'll be places when she'll need to be restrained, that's why Nineteen is there. Eamon, Tara will be ten times as strong as you are. You'll need to stay back out of the way so you don't get hurt. Understand?"

"I understand. Jeannie ..."

"Go on, get back in there. You've got some explaining to do to your wife. Do it, Eamon, keep her distracted as much as possible when she's lucid then get out of the way when she loses it, and she will lose it, many times. Go on now." He nodded then left the office.

"Now, Lilly, tell me you held back a few of those berries we sent you to collect."

"No Captain. You gave me strict orders to deliver them all to Dr. Reilly, so I did as you commanded."

"Oh yeah? Then what's that smug little grin for?"

"You didn't say anything about the actual bushes. My father and I have several growing happily in Hydroponics. I can have berries for you in about three days."

Jeannie leaned back in the chair and chuckled with delight. "Lilly, you're the best. As soon as those berries are even close to ripe get them to Carla. The new SUVI will need them by then."

"Understood, Captain."

"You seem pretty confident this woman will survive, Jeannie."

"I am, Carla. Every sense I have is telling me she'll survive and become a full SUVI. The big problem right now is the virus. Did any of it escape into the rest of the ship, or did we manage to contain it in the lab. Once Tara has passed through the change the lab will have to be cleansed.

"Mandy, if you look closely through the transparent doors of the lab you can see the virus container. Is there any way you can get a lock on it and transport it off the ship?"

"If I can see it I can scan its location then go to Transport and do the deed. Where shall I send it?"

"Open space, as far off the ship as possible, then get Linsey to take you out in her little ship and use the weapon on it, blow it to hell and back."

"Jeannie?"

"Sweetheart, that damned virus wiped out over nine thousand colonists on Elysium. I don't want to take any chances of it getting back on this ship. It was active for moments only in Eamon's system. I can't trust him at the best of times, and I don't want to take any chances with this thing."

Amanda nodded but it was Carla who voiced the surprise. "You can't trust him, Jeannie?"

"Dr. Reilly is a real independent thinker, Carla. I'm sure he'll be fine once Tara has recovered, but until then I want him watched. If she doesn't make it who knows what he might do? Keep an eye on him and learn how he made that antidote. If it truly works as well as it appears then I want the whole ship's complement inoculated.

"Lilly, you and your father are on berry production. We're going to need a lot of them."

"Yes Ma'am."

"Mandy, once Tara has passed through the change Thirteen can help her to adjust to her new abilities, but she'll need you to help her adjust to interacting with the rest of the humans again. Time has passed without her, her body and brain will be changed, and you're the one with the most experience in helping a SUVI through this adjustment period."

Amanda smiled and gave Jeannie's hand a gentle squeeze. "I'll help her all I can, I promise. Right now I have a dangerous virus to transport off the ship." A quick pat on the shoulder for Jeannie then she walked away.

"That's my cue," smiled Lilly. "With your permission, Captain." Jeannie nodded, and Lilly left to speak with her father and his supervisor in Hydroponics.

As they were left alone, Jeannie turned back to Carla. "Talk to me, Chief of Medical Staff, did any of that virus get out of the lab?"

"No."

"You sound pretty sure."

"Dr. Reilly sealed the door behind him when he went into the lab. I set the seals before you went through, so you passed through the filters on the way in and again on the way out. Dr. Reilly had already calibrated the filters to detect and destroy the virus. I double checked that setting then scanned the whole area out here while you were inside.

"The SUVI went in through the filters and you came out through the same. As soon as Mandy completes her transport I'll scan the lab from here. With luck, only Tara will have a live virus. Jeannie, that damned virus terrifies me. I'll do everything in my power to make sure it doesn't escape.

"Now, can you tell me why you don't trust Dr. Reilly?"

"As soon as he learned I was different, and how I got that way, he was keenly interested. Remember how he sent you out on Explorer One instead of going himself? He was utterly focused on the berries I'd given him. That caught my attention.

"Next, when we recovered the container of virus from Jonah Thornton, Eamon insisted on keeping it on the Reacher. That concerned me. The tale of his deathly ill wife came out when I gave Linsey control of all things alien and he objected so strongly.

"I then understood what was happening with Eamon. He's devoted his entire career, his life, to finding a cure for Tara. It became his entire life's focus, his reason to exist, his religion. Like any true religious zealot, he would do anything, regardless of the cost, to see her recover.

"Over the years he hid her on this ship, lied to Captain Baris, to me, disobeyed orders, unnecessarily risked lives, all your lives, in the mad desire to achieve his quest. My arrival on the ship, and the information I brought with me, gave him renewed focus, renewed hope."

"Oh my god, Jeannie, I can see it all clearly now that you've explained it. Jake was right. He suspected all along that Dr. Reilly was up to something. So, what happens now? What will you do to him?"

"Nothing at all, Carla. It's already been done. I've removed him to research and put you in charge of medical. Carla, Eamon's still the best doctor we have. I need you to pick his brain every chance you get, learn whatever he's willing to teach. He can't hurt us anymore now, and his driving motivation has been achieved. It's my hope that he'll now turn his attention to passing along his great experience, his vast knowledge gained over a lifetime, to you."

"Yeah, he's been mentoring me, teaching me, but it's a tough learning curve. I'll do my best here, Jeannie, you know I will."

"Yes indeed, the right person for the job."

* * * * *

"Mendalo, let's go, we just got a call to action from Commander Drake."

"Commander Linsey? Are we not waiting for Lady Eighteen?" The small man looked somewhat perplexed. He was a newly revived Earalithian, trying to fully grasp the human/SUVI command structure. There didn't seem to be a lot of structure to it, but it worked for them.

"No, she's on another mission and this won't take long. You can operate the weapons of the ship, right?"

"Yes, I am familiar with those weapons."

"Good, then you're my guy, let's go." She led the way to Ship 87643 in the cargo bay.

"Ship greets Captain da Silva and officer Mendalo. Are we making another test flight?"

"Not this time friend, Ship, we have a quick mission. Da Silva to control."

"Control."

"Requesting launch."

"Granted. Doors opening. Doors are open, Ship, you are clear to launch."

"Thank you, Control. Ship, have you received the target coordinates."

"Ship has coordinates. Releasing weapons control to Officer Mendalo."

"Gunner?"

"Target acquired, Captain," chuckled the grinning man at the controls.

"Fire when ready, Gunner."

"Firing. Target destroyed, Captain da Silva."

"Thank you, Chief Gunner. Commander da Silva to Commander Drake."

* * * * *

Outside the medical office, Amanda was on her comms. "Drake to Three, are you on Explorer?"

"Three here, Commander. Yes, I'm on the ship, what do you need?"

"I'm sending you the coordinates of a certain small container. I need you to transport it out into space, well away from Reacher. When that's done, send the coordinates of its new location to Commander da Silva aboard Ship 87643."

"Understood." There was a moment of waiting then Amanda grinned as she watched through the glass while the container vanished from the lab in a flash of light. "Three to Commander Drake. Mission Complete."

"Thank you, Three. Commander Drake to Commander da Silva. Do you have the coordinates?"

"da Silva here. Ship launching now. Got 'em Commander." Again Amanda waited, longer this time. Finally, she got the call. "Commander da Silva to Commander Drake. Mission accomplished; target destroyed. Ship returning."

"Well done, Linsey, and thank you."

Amanda returned to Carla's office. "It's done, Jeannie. The virus has been transported away from the ship then destroyed."

"Thank you, sweet Mandy. I can finally stop worrying about that threat."

* * * * *

In the healing bay a wild-eyed woman fought like a tigress, but all to no avail. The huge man who held her gently was like a mountain, silent, immovable, stone, uncaring, unyielding, and impervious to pain.

Nearby two women helped an older man sit up. "Looks like he's coming around, Four. He's a bit addled, but he'll be fine."

"Man doesn't listen well, does he, Eighteen? We told him to keep back."

"Oh dear god, I hurt. What hit me?"

"Your wife," grinned SUVI Four. "Next time we tell you to get back, get the hell back."

"Come take her, Eighteen, her fever's rising again, the fight's gone out of her."

The small woman rose and went to where the big man held the woman still. She was feverish now and lying limply in his arms. Gently she took the deathly ill woman from his arms. "Hush now, Eighteen's got you, Tara. I know it hurts, honey, I know. Hush now and snuggle into my arms. I'll hold you until the pain passes."

She was still crooning softly as Nineteen helped the battered doctor to his feet. "It's been so long since anyone had gotten infected, I'd almost forgotten how powerful it can be."

"Is it always like this?"

"No, this case is special. There was no one to help any of us through, we had to survive on our own. I was the last to manage it."

"How much longer will this go on?"

"A couple more days, three at most."

"What do you think of her chances?"

"Actually, Doctor, I like her chances. The fevers are slowing down and she's getting stronger."

"So I noticed."

"You were warned to stay back. Any signs of joint pain, confusion?"

"No, just pain in my face from where she hit me."

"Then it looks like your antidote worked. That's a good thing."

"Thanks, I think. I just wish ..." He was interrupted by the ping of his comm unit. "Reilly here."

"Dr. Reilly, Linsey is here with a basket of berries."

"Keep them cool, Carla. Nineteen says they're of no use now until she's through the change."

"Understood."

Chapter 13

A New Order

For three days Brandon Hoffman ran the ship, Emmet Jones ran the bridge, and all the department heads went about their business while trying to stay out of the captain's way. For her part, Jeannie spent most of her waking hours in Medical, pacing.

She didn't enter the lab where Tara Reilly was passing through the change, she didn't want to risk the virus getting loose. Tara's helpers were a haggard looking group by the time she settled down. Finally, it was over.

"Her fever's broken completely," said Four. "I believe we're clear. It's time for the final test."

Eighteen nodded and reached for the comm. "Coming out for the berries now."

"I'll bring them in."

"Very good, Five."

Jeannie stepped through the airlock to see her tired crew sitting there with a disheveled Tara Reilly in the middle. "Hello, Tara, how are you feeling?"

"Wait, I know you. You comforted me when I was hurting so badly. Please forgive me, I'm struggling to focus, but the pain is gone, and I actually feel stronger than I have in years."

"Very good. Now, tell me a bit about yourself."

"Yes, of course. I'm on a ship, aren't I, and you're the captain. You're also a SUVI, or did I imagine that part? No, wait, you're not human, neither are these people who helped me. I ... I ... I'm different too, not human either, but like you people. What did you do to me? So sorry, having trouble staying focused, need to be somewhere ... somewhere with the others ..."

"Here, Tara, eat these berries, they'll help you clear your head."

"Okay, sure, if you say so."

She began to eat the berries and discovered her appetite had returned. While she feasted, Jeannie turned to Dr. Reilly. "Eamon, how's she doing?"

"Better than average." He groaned as he levered himself into a better sitting position. "Me, on the other hand, I'll need a few days to recover, and the bruising will take longer to go down."

"I did warn you to stay back."

"You did, but I had no real idea."

"She get out of hand a few times, Four?"

"She did, Five, but not as bad as you did. Even as a ten-year-old, you managed to break a few bones before your fevers broke."

"Why are you people using numbers instead of names?"

"Think, Tara, remember what I told you when you first awakened."

"Yes, yes I remember. You said there were only nineteen survivors of the virus so now you use the number in which you survived. You were the fifth survivor."

"Yes, and you are the twentieth, Tara. How are you feeling now?"

"My mind is clearing. That need to be somewhere is receding. What is that?"

"That is your SUVI need to join the herd, your own kind. You are here with us now, so that should pass. In the coming days a teacher will come to you, he is Thirteen. He will help you discover your SUVI nature and abilities. A woman will come as well. She will help you learn how to interact with the humans again."

"Interact with the humans?"

"Yes, you're full SUVI now, stronger, faster, and your mind will work differently, your needs and desires will be different. How are you feeling now?"

"Much better, thank you. My mind is clearing, I don't have to fight to remain focused."

"Wonderful. So, SUVI 20, who are you? Who will you be? Will you be Tara Reilly, SUVI 20, or Suvi-Tara?"

"I don't understand."

"When I first returned to the Reacher as an adult I changed my name from SUVI 5 to Suvi-jean Sorenson. I was Jeannie Sorenson before I became infected. However, the rest of the SUVI have decided to retain their number as their official name. Your three companions who helped you through the fevers are Four, Eighteen, and Nineteen."

"Can I just be Tara now until I absorb some of what's happened to me?"

"Yes, you can. Eamon, what do your scanners say?"

"We're clear, Jeannie. There's not a trace of live virus anywhere in here. I'm picking it up from the five of you, but it's dormant."

Smiling, Jeannie reached for her comm. "Carla, we're clear in here. If it's clear out there you can release the lockdown."

"Understood, releasing lockdown." There was a hiss then the airtight seals around the door released. "Eamon, take Tara home and let her get reoriented to the ship, get her some clean clothes, etc. Once she had a good meal and feels ready, send for Amanda and Thirteen. They'll help her adjust to who and what she's become."

"If possible, Captain, I'd prefer my own quarters for now. Dr. Reilly and I have much to discuss."

Jeannie chuckled at that. "All right, Tara. I'll get someone to help you." She reached for her comm. "Sorenson to Commander Drake."

"Amanda here."

"SUVI 20 is awake and ready to start a new life. Can you come to Medical and help her out?"

"On my way."

"Tara, Amanda is the one who helped me re-assimilate into life on a ship. She'll also introduce you to Thirteen. Ah, there she is now. Amanda my delight, this woman is Tara, SUVI 20. Tara, Amanda will see to your needs. We'll all clear out now and let Carla put her infirmary back in order."

"Hi Tara, come with me, we'll get you set up in quarters. Do you want to be close to Dr. Reilly?"

"Yes, but not too close."

"I understand. Right this way." Amanda led the way to the crew quarters section of the ship. "This is Dr. Reilly's quarters, and we have an empty two doors down. Will this do?"

"This will be fine."

Amanda opened the door and stepped inside, inviting Tara to follow. "Take a look around, is everything familiar to you?"

"Somewhat."

"Okay, I can show you, or I can leave so you can experiment on your own, come back later."

"Can you give me an hour?"

"You got it." Amanda smiled and left her there.

The new SUVI 20 sighed and began to explore, luxuriated in the shower, then dressed in the new ship's uniform provided. A soft knock came on the door.

It was Amanda. "If you'd rather I come back later I could ..."

"No, please stay. You're human, aren't you?"

"Yes, I'm human."

"But I'm not, not anymore, am I?"

"No, you're SUVI now."

"Can you tell me what that means?"

"SUVI, survivor of unknown viral infection. It means that you have managed to survive a transformation that killed thousands, you've defied the odds, the virus, and come out stronger. Your body is now a lot stronger, you'll heal faster, and your brain will function differently."

"There, that's the part I'm concerned about. What do you know about that?"

"Well, it took me a while to wrap my head around some of it, but it looks a bit like this: the brain of a SUVI has compartmentalized into three main process sections. One part focuses on survival, one on task, and one on place within the group.

"Thirteen will help you with this until you can basically focus on three different things at once. Linsey calls it being a functional scatter brain, but I see you folk as the ultimate multi-taskers."

Tara laughed at that. "I can see the advantages. Amanda, I'll confess, I haven't felt this good since before I got sick. I feel stronger than ever."

"You are stronger than ever before. It'll take a bit of experimenting for you to get comfortable with your new strength. I expect you'll break a few things, bend a few things, and maybe give yourself a few bruises before you get it worked out."

"Yeah, I guess. Speaking of working it out, I suppose I should see a counsellor."

"Oh?"

"I have some stuff to work out, as you might guess. Is there a ship's counsellor?"

"We had one until two years ago."

"Oh?"

"Yes. He committed suicide, transported himself off the ship. Is there anything I can do to help?"

"Listen to me bitch, whine, and complain?"

Amanda grinned and sank into a chair. "Go for it, sister."

"Sure, why not," sighed Tara as she too plopped into a chair. "Look, first let me say how grateful I am to you and all the medical staff. I also owe your captain a debt of gratitude. I came out of cryo, sick, weak, in terrible pain, and totally confused. She was there, held me gently and tried to explain what was happening, but it was so hard to focus through the pain."

"As I understand it, that was part of the virus at work."

"Yes, that's what Four said. It took me a while to fully grasp that it wasn't my father-in-law there, but my husband, thirty years older. He'd put me in cryo like another of his lab rats. I'd made peace with the world; I was ready to die. You see, there was no cure, we knew that, but Eamon wouldn't let go. He must have sedated me then put me in cryo.

"Anyway, I woke up on a ship instead of in a hospital, sicker than ever, everything strange, crazy, an old man for a husband, and ... I mean, it's thirty years later, my husband is old, my planet is dead, and I'm on a ship halfway across the galaxy. It's a lot to take in, you know?"

"I'm sure it is. Tara, have you ever met an alien before?"

Tara raised an elbow at her. "Apparently, I am the alien."

Amanda was grinning at her now. "I want you to meet somebody." She reached for her comms. "Commander Drake to Antha."

"Here, Commander."

"Antha, can you come to my current location?"

"On my way."

Amanda smiled at Tara's questioning look. "Antha is an Earalithian woman. She had her lover froze to death when their planet suffered a catastrophic event. We found them and revived them. As near as we can tell they were frozen there for several hundred thousand years."

"You're not serious."

"Oh yes I am. I think you two will be able to relate quite well." A soft tap came at the door. "There she is now. Enter, Antha."

Tara was slightly taken aback at the appearance of the small woman who stepped through the door. "You wanted to see me, Commander?"

"Yes, Antha. This is Tara, our new SUVI. She was in cryo sleep for many years then awakened to a very different world. I thought you might be better able to relate to her situation than I can."

"Yes, I'm sure I can. Hello, Tara. May I touch you?"

"What? Why?"

"I won't harm you. It's the manner in which my kind greet new people when we meet for the first time."

"Well, okay, I guess."

Smiling shyly Antha approached and reached to lightly grip Tara's shoulders. She touched her forehead to Tara's. "I greet you in friendship, SUVI 20. I am Antha, companion to Morthel, citizen of Starship Reacher, friend of Commander Drake."

Tara carefully held the small woman's shoulders. "I'm Tara Reilly, now SUVI 20. I accept your friendship, Antha, with gratitude."

Antha smiled and stepped back. "How can I serve?"

"Amanda tells me you were in a frozen sleep a lot longer than I was."

"Yes, that is true. It's difficult to awaken in a strange place with unknown people all around you, your world gone, your home vanished, your place in the order of things no longer valid."

"Wow, you truly do understand. How do you cope, Antha?"

"As my mentor, Commander Drake, tells me, one day at a time. Face each day with a determination to make a new friend, serve the greater good, and take pleasure in that service."

"You know, not many of my species would agree with that, but for some reason it truly resonates with me on a deep level."

"It should," smiled Antha. "It's the driving force of your new species, the SUVI. It's what you are now. I've spent a lot of time with Linsey and Eighteen, plus I've watched Amanda with Captain Sorenson. I can see the difference in the two species, human and SUVI. Each has its own merits and difficulties. Add in my own species, and Reacher becomes an interesting place to be."

"So, are you alone here as well?"

"No, there are ten more Earalith, yet, when I went to sleep there were thousands of planets filled with Earalith. For all we know now, we may well be the last of our kind, even as the people of Reacher are the last of theirs.

"Tell me of your experience."

"Oh, well, I worked three jobs to put my husband through medical school but became ill shortly after he graduated. Eamon had already signed us up for colonization before I admitted I was getting sick. He wanted to stay with me, but I was deteriorating so fast. They said I might have six months to live, but the ship was leaving in four.

"Knowing I was dying, I asked for the final cocktail."

"The suicide drink?"

"Yes, Commander Drake. I didn't want Eamon to throw away his whole career, his dream, just to spend three months watching me die in pain. He brought it to me then held me as I fell asleep. The next thing you know, I wake up in worse shape, sicker than before, a man I thought was my father-in-law standing over me, and your captain facing his anger.

"I hurt like you couldn't imagine, but the captain held me, comforted me, told me what had happened, then sent for people to help me. Somehow I managed to live through it, became an alien with super powers."

Amanda was grinning. "What kind of superpowers do you have?" That brought a laugh from Tara.

"Commander, thank you for that. I can't remember when I last laughed. Yes, I'm told I will have special abilities. There's a man who's supposed to help me discover what they might be, but at the moment, I have no idea at all."

"Thirteen. He's a tough customer, Tara, but he's good. He'll push you, but if you pay attention to what he says, everything has a lesson, everything is important."

"You like him."

"I do. He's on my crew, and invaluable to me. At my lowest ebb he got in my face, rubbed my fur the wrong way, and taught me some very important things. I'll send him to you when you're ready. Take a few days to relax and get the feel of the new body first."

"Yes, I do need to adjust to this. I'm almost too strong, but for the first time in forever I'm not in any pain."

"That's good to hear." Antha patted her hand. "Now, tell me what's really got you messed up."

"What makes you think I'm messed up?"

"Your eyes are still amber. When a SUVI is on full alert or in distress, their eyes turn amber."

"Well crap, there goes Friday night poker."

"Excuse me?"

"Sorry, Antha. It's a gambling game where it's very important to hide your emotions and reactions from your opponents."

Antha giggled at that. "Oh yes, that's no game for a SUVI to play. So, what was that bothering you again?"

"All right, Miss Relentless. It's Eamon, my husband. He disobeyed my wishes, tricked me, infected me with a deadly virus, and then turned out to be sixty years old instead of thirty. What am I supposed to do about him?"

Amanda leaned back in her chair and gave Tara a gentle smile. "Yes, Suvi-jean will tell you he doesn't take orders well. On the other hand, he risked life and limb as well as his whole career, convinced his captain to smuggle you on board the Far Star, and again onto the Reacher. He dedicated his entire existence to saving your life, restoring you.

"He could have accepted your decision, chosen another companion at any time over the last thirty years, but he didn't. The man loves you madly and has worked tirelessly to bring you back.

"Right now he knows the captain has the power, and should, take his scalp, that he risked the entirety of his own species in the attempt to heal you, and he knows he succeeded, but you're no longer human, no longer his beloved Tara. He awakened his lover in that lab, but the woman sitting in this room isn't her, she's SUVI 20.

"I guess the question now is, how much of Tara Reilly is still inside there? Does she want to reconcile with him, or what?"

"I should go talk to him, huh?"

"When you're ready," smiled Antha as she patted Tara's hand.

"Yeah, I guess I should. Guys, I can't thank you enough for the therapy session."

"All our pleasure. So, Commander Drake, is this the part where we all go to the mess and eat too many desserts?"

Both Amanda and Tara laughed. Amanda grinned and shook a finger at the smiling Earalithian. "Antha, you've been hanging around with Linsey and Eighteen entirely too much. All right, I'm in. Tara?"

"Sure, why not. I've eaten nothing but pills and worse for far too long. Let's do it."

They had barely settled at the table when a voice sounded behind them. "What's this? A party at the captain's table, but the captain wasn't invited?"

Amanda grinned with delight. "Is the captain prepared to sacrifice herself in the destruction of these desserts?"

"The captain will prepare herself for battle and be right back."

They all chuckled as Suvi-jean walked away then returned with a plateful of delights for herself. "All right, ladies, what are we celebrating, the arrival of a new SUVI perhaps?"

Tara smiled shyly as she replied. "You could call it that. I'd like to think of it as a new life for Tara." She sighed and gazed at her hands. "I guess that's not right, is it? Tara's gone, never to return. Whoever I am now, it isn't Tara. Perhaps I'll do like the others. Call me SUVI 20, Twenty for short."

"Are you certain?"

"Yes, Captain, I am. I also need to thank you for all you've done for me. You held and comforted me when I woke up in such terrible pain. You sent in the troops to protect me from myself while the virus changed me."

"No thanks are necessary, Twenty. I'm just so thrilled to have you with us."

"You really are, aren't you? Why, Captain? What makes me so special?"

Jeannie sighed and laid down her fork, then smiled at Tara. "You are so much more than special, Twenty. All SUVI are special, but you so much more so. You have never felt the lash of the pain collar, you will never know a single day of slavery, you will never be held back because your controllers fear what you are, what you might become.

"From the moment you walked out of the infirmary you have been free to explore who and what you are, free to become what you will, whatever you want to be. You are the first freemade SUVI, and I hope you will be the last. It is my hope the future SUVI will be born to us in the more human fashion."

"You said slavery, were the SUVI slaves. How did that happen if they are created by a virus?"

Amanda smiled and patted Twenty's hand. "I'll send Thirteen to you tomorrow. He'll give you the history of the SUVI plus help you figure out your unique abilities."

"Unique abilities, like how I know the captain's hiding something, but is busting to share, and how I know Eamon just walked in, but went to a corner and sat with his back to us, even though I can't see him."

"Yeah, things like that," grinned Amanda. "So, captain, what are you hiding from us?"

"I can't tell you that, I'm hiding it from you."

"Suvi-jean, you're getting way too good at this teasing thing."

"Okay, I'll share. I think we're about done here at Frigid and should soon be moving on. I just want to organize and finalize a few things before we set sail again. I'll elaborate more at the next senior staff meeting."

"And that sounds like you folks are about to start discussing top secret stuff that I don't need to know about. If you'll excuse me, I should go introduce myself to Tara's husband."

"You mean, your husband."

"No, Commander Drake, Tara's husband. I'm not that woman. Yes, she's a big part of me, but only a part, and he needs to understand that."

"All right, do your thing, girl." They watched her walk to the table where Eamon Reilly sat alone. "Jeannie, will she be okay, do you think?"

"Yes, she'll be fine now. Did you notice how fast she's evolving? A few hours ago she just wanted to find quarters alone and hide out, now she's ready to face a tough situation head on."

"You knew this would happen."

"No, but I hoped it would. You see, no SUVI before her has had the opportunity to just evolve and explore themselves like she's doing. It'll be fun to watch her grow."

* * * * *

"Howdy stranger, mind if I sit down."

Eamon Reilly sighed with relief as a smile spread across his face. She'd just used the first words he'd ever spoken to her. He replied with her original response. "Not at all, as long as you do it somewhere else." Her laughter was full and rich. It had been over thirty years since he'd last heard it and it brought tears to his eyes.

"You must be the eminent Dr. Eamon Reilly who created me. Greetings, Dr., I'm SUVI 20; call me Twenty."

"You're going with the SUVI designation?"

"It's what I am, a SUVI, the twentieth survivor."

"All right then, Twenty it is. So, can we talk?"

"That's why I'm here."

"Will you hear me out?"

"Yes."

"Tara, sorry, Twenty, I just couldn't part with you, I couldn't. I couldn't accept that I wouldn't be able to beat it, find a cure. Olga Volkov recruited me for her ship, and I accepted on condition I could bring you on board. She agreed.

"When we got back to find Earth destroyed, the captains decided to blend the works of us into one group and Olga lost the draw. Frank

Baris won and the Reacher became the one ship, Olga was assigned First Officer, and as such she was able to help me smuggle you on board.

"I worked for years, tried everything I could think of, but failed, and then Suvi-jean Sorenson came riding onto the ship on a dinosaur. She slew the beast with a dagger, then over the following months took over the ship. That was what saved me, and you.

"Frank would have shot me and given you a decent burial in space. Jeannie fired me as Chief of Medical and appointed me as Chief of Medical Research, told me to make you top priority. She'd already given me the magic berries, and then captured the virus.

"Tara, had it worked according to plan, I'd have given you the antidote before the virus had a chance to change you, but I got infected, and Jeannie gave me the injection that was meant for you. Because of that you went through hell, and I'm deeply sorry for that."

"Don't be because I'm not. Look, Eamon, Tara was finished, dying and ready to go. She begged you to let her go. What you did, along with the captain's actions, created me. Yes, I went through hell, it was a tough birth, but I'm here, a SUVI, and according to the captain, unique among them."

"Tara, I ..."

"I know, you're sorry; you said that already. So what are you sorry about, Tara's finally gone and you have to let go? Sorry that you ..."

"No, dammit, I'm sorry that I lost the woman that I loved more than life."

"But you did, and now it's time to move on, find another companion." He just sat staring at her, then he noticed the tiny grin playing at her lips. "So, I'm single, want to hang out together?"

He laughed with delight as she used another line from their original meeting. "Tara, can you mean that, after all that's happened?"

"Twenty, remember, call me Twenty. Yes, Eamon, I truly do mean that. I still love you, dummy, but you messed me up, I'm all different now. I want us to start over fresh and see if it still works. You game?"

"Oh yes indeed, I'm game. We do this at your pace, Lady Twenty. Where do we start?"

"We already have. Look, I do need to get some rest and then I need one of the girls to show me how things work on this giant ship, then we can start spending time together, lots of it, you know, if you can. You're getting on now, and ..."

"Oh woman, that's going to cost you."

They were both grinning. "Come on, sailor, walk me home."

Chapter 14

Ready to Jump

The senior staff gathered at the captain's call, including the commanders of the small ships as well as the elected president of the former grounders, now called passengers, Miriam Holbrooke. Suvi-jean smiled as she sank into her chair. "People, I believe we're ready to set sail again, but I want to make certain. Report."

"Things aboard the Reacher have been busy, Captain, but I believe we're under control. We've got tons of salvage, new crew, new ships, and lots of new tech. People are working overtime on all of it, but I think Frigid has revealed all that she can. We could deal with what we have while in transit."

"Thank you, Brandon. Amanda, your assessment?"

"Me? Oh, yes, of course. The Explorer has searched the planet twice over and our Earalithian crewman believes we will find no further intact bodies. Explorer and crew are ready to set sail."

"Excellent. Grandfather?"

"As you all know, Recovery took some damage, but has been fully repaired. I believe her captain will be back at the helm within days, and our Chief of Salvage believes we'll find nothing more of value here. Now he's all excited about getting a look at the next planet."

"Chief of Salvage?"

"Chance Morita. The man has mad skills, so Olga promoted him."

Suvi-jean smiled and nodded her approval. "Carla?"

"We're all good in medical. Commander Volkov is ready to go, but I want to run a few final tests just to be doubly sure. We keep checking, but no sign of the virus anywhere. We're ready to go if you are."

"Engineering?"

"Ah, Jeannie, I can't tell you how much fun I'm having. We've got a hold full of magic for me to explore. Okay, where we are, both Explorer and Recovery have full Earalithian shields, Ship 87643 is good as new, and that ore hauler we salvaged is being refitted and christened Recovery Two. It'll take a while, but we've got everything we need to complete the job.

"The energy shields for Reacher are being installed as we speak. With luck they'll work just as we planned."

"How's Dorind working out?"

"The wee lad's a wealth of knowledge and experience, we work well together."

"Good to know. Linsey."

"All things alien are under control, Captain. We now have several crew speaking passable Earalith, the Earalithians are finding ways to contribute, to fit in and make friends. I've left the tech stuff to Engineering and concentrated on ways to help the newly awakened people, and to develop possible scenarios and protocols for meeting more new species.

"Antha seems to have appointed herself Ship's Counsellor and is doing a brisk business."

"Seriously?" Linsey nodded. "All right, see if you can get her an office next to yours and ... oh hell, if it's already working, let it work. Just tell her I'm pleased and to carry on as she sees fit. Sheila?"

"All appears to be quiet from a Security standpoint, Captain. We're ready to sail if you are."

"Emmet?"

"Bridge crew ready to sail at any time, Captain."

"Excellent. Medical Research?"

Eamon Reilly almost looked startled. "Me? Oh, well, I've been studying both the Earalithian and SUVI genome, trying to see if they are compatible with humans."

"You mean reproductively compatible?"

"Yes." He blushed deeply then pointed a finger at Amanda. "Amanda Drake, I truly curse the day you taught Captain Sorenson how to tease a human."

Amanda grinned as she replied. "She is getting much better at it, isn't she?"

"She's killing me. Yes, Captain, I was exploring the possibilities. I believe it's possible for a human/SUVI pairing to produce a child, but it is highly unlikely. Actually, the Earalith and SUVI are a better match."

"Seriously?"

Eamon sighed and melted back into his chair. "Yes, I'm serious. Human and SUVI are possible, Human and Earalith possible but unlikely, Earalith and SUVI have good chances, but same species pairings have the best chances, of course."

"Eamon, I'd really like to revisit this at a later time. Keep at it because this research may be the means to our eventual survival.

"Miriam, is everything all right with the passengers?"

"My people will be thrilled that we're on the move in the right direction. We're ready to go, Captain."

"So, we're all ready to go exploring?"

They all chuckled at that. "We're ready, Captain," grinned the First Officer, "just waiting for you to give the order."

"So be it. Second Officer, return to the bridge and aim us at the original target planet." He rose to his feet, and with an easy "Aye Captain" limped from the room.

"All right, people, what did Commander Jones not tell me?"

Linsey laughed with delight. "Ettelan must be on shift."

"Linsey, who is Ettelan?"

"He's one of the Earalithians we revived. He's a ship's pilot, but his ship was damaged on impact and he was put into the lottery. Like Morthel, he didn't get a seat so had to remain behind. When I found out I took him to the bridge and asked Commander Jones to show him around.

"I waited, expecting it would be a short tour at best, but they started talking pilot stuff, and after an hour, I gave up and left them to it. Next day I learned Ettelan had joined the bridge crew, replacing a pilot who wanted to retire. He must be on shift right now."

"Linsey, that's wonderful. It pleases me that you've managed to find ways to help the Earalithians to fit in. Well done.

"Lady Amanda, care to join me on the bridge as we set sail?"

"Love to, Captain."

"Then let us away. Meeting adjourned people. You might as well relax a bit, even with the new modifications to the engines it'll take us a week or two to arrive." With that she took Amanda's hand and led her out onto the bridge.

"Captain on the bridge!"

"As you were. Commander Jones, are we ready?"

"Ready at all stations, Captain."

"I see you have a new pilot, Commander. Why wasn't I informed of this?"

The small man at the pilot's station looked up fearfully, then relaxed as the captain's companion winked at him, a smile playing at her lips. The bridge commander also winked at him. "I'm sorry, Captain. I just assumed all crew appointments would be relayed to you through the First Officer."

"Ah-huh." Suvi-jean lost her attempt to hide her grin. "Very well then, Pilot, are you ready?"

"Aye, Captain. Course is laid in, ship is re-oriented to new course, engines are charged and ready."

"Ship's status, Second Officer?"

"All hatches closed and locked down, Captain. All departments reported in readiness."

"Excellent. Pilot, hit it."

With a grin of delight, the small man moved a lever and the gigantic ship shuddered slightly then vanished from her orbit about the frozen dead world they'd called Frigid. Travelling at unimaginable speeds, the Reacher hurtled toward the nearest star system and another planet waiting to be explored.

"Ship is underway, Captain."

"Thank you, Commander Jones. You have the bridge." With a wink at the Earalithian pilot, she turned and led Amanda from the bridge, heading for their quarters.

As they relaxed inside, Amanda brought her a container of water then snuggled into the chair beside her. "Jeannie honey, what's bugging you? We've set sail for a new planet; this is the part where you're supposed to be pleased and happy. What's going on?"

"I don't know, Mandy. I've checked in with Thirteen and Eighteen, but they can't get a handle on it either. We're going to hit trouble at that new planet, it has something to do with the Earalith, but we have no idea what that trouble might be. Worse yet, we dare not bypass the planet. We'd have a riot on our hands if we try."

"Yeah, the crew might be okay with it, but the passengers would have a fit, that's for sure. What are you going to do?"

"The SUVI and I are all training, honing our skills and abilities as best we can. There's not much else we can do until we get there and discover how the danger will present itself."

"So, you have nothing else to do except sit here and worry?"

"Sadly, that appears to be it."

"Hmm. This seems to be one of those places where I have to do my job."

"Do your job?"

"Yes, my job of keeping you distracted from all the things that distress you." With a grin of mischief, Amanda began to lightly nibble on Suvi-jean's ear lobe.

"Oh gods, yes, Mandy. You're so very good at your job." She got no further as Amanda sealed her lips with a soft loving kiss.

Chapter 15

Making Ready

The mighty Reacher hurtled through space, bearing down on the planet of hope. As she neared the star system, feelings were mixed throughout the ship. The former colonists were ready to try again, but they were no longer as young as they had been when they were dropped on Elysium. Many were nearing retirement age, and there were far too few younger people among them.

A recruiting drive was started to gather more potential colonists from the crew, but there were surprisingly few young people interested. Bemused and troubled, Miriam Holbrooke and two others asked for a meeting with the senior staff to discuss the problem. The captain also asked her grandfather and Jake White to sit in on the meeting.

"Okay, we're all here, what's on your mind, folks?" asked the captain.

Miriam sighed and addressed the question directly. "Captain, we have a huge problem. As you are all too aware, the original colony had a population of ten thousand souls. There are only about seven hundred of us left, and far too many of us are reaching the age when we don't have the physical strength required for this sort of venture."

"Yes, I heard you've been recruiting from the crew."

"We have, but without any real success."

Olga Volkov sat forward and gazed at the captain. "Wait, wasn't the idea that we all colonize the planet? That was why we returned to Elysium, wasn't it?"

Frank Baris sighed and studied his hands. "Yes, that was the idea, our idea, the five captains. However, we neglected to poll the crew, discover their opinion on the subject. As Miriam and company are now learning, most of the crew aren't interested in settling down to farm, they're explorers at heart.

"What do you think, Jeannie? You're the captain, this is your decision to make."

Suvi-jean sighed and leaned back in her chair as she spoke. "People, I will now confess myself to you. When I was made captain, I vowed to find you all a planet you could colonize, but once that colony was established, I planned to take the SUVI and friends aboard the Explorer and seek out a place of our own.

"However, I can see the Explorer will be far too small for the task. I'll admit I've enjoyed our exploration and success at Frigid. I'll land those who want to colonize, but I'm hoping there'll be enough explorers like me to take the Reacher and go poking around for the sake of learning what we can learn."

One of the men with Miriam Holbrooke leaped to his feet. "No. You can't take the ship and just leave. Look what happened on Elysium. What will happen if ..."

He got no further as Jake's hand fell heavily on his shoulder. "That's enough, now sit down and pay attention. My friend, Captain Sorenson is in charge of the Reacher, and the Reacher goes wherever she decides to take it. Point number two, as a SUVI, the captain is well aware of what happened on Elysium."

"Easy, Jake, he gets it. My friend, Jake's right, I'm all too aware of what happened on Elysium, and I'm also aware that, if the ship had still been in the area when the first migration swept through, thousands of lives could have been saved."

The man sat back down, so the captain went on. "Jake, you've been taking an informal survey for me. Are you getting a sense of where we stand?"

"Captain, over half the crew would rather stay in space, go exploring. That's more than enough people to man the Reacher plus the smaller ships."

"So, you're saying half our crew could be persuaded to become colonists?"

"I do, Captain. It's the same old story, way too many crew and not enough useful things to do, little chance of advancement, etc. On the planet they'd have better chances."

"If that's true, why is Miriam having so much trouble getting recruits?"

Jake chuckled as he resumed his seat. "As one man told me, not realizing who I am, I'd be a raw newbie, no useful skills so I'd be used for labor, building homes, digging irrigation and sanitation trenches. Being told you're useless and won't be allowed near any of the important jobs isn't very appealing.

"I also overheard two men talking, wondering why the sky-riders were even being considered for the colony. They assured each other that grounders would get first choice of the jobs as well as the home sites, and they'd be damned if they would grow crops just to have them beamed up for use on the ship.

"Captain, you've made great strides in reconciling the two factions, crew and passengers, but there's still a lot of bad blood out there, and people aren't too sure they want to volunteer for that. Yes, at least half the crew would be willing to go down, but not under those circumstances."

"Your recommendations?"

"Little sister, I've got nothing here. I have no idea at all how to fix any of this."

"Well, people, I'm actually quite pleased to know I'll have a crew for the ship, but Miriam, you've got your work cut out for you. By Jake's figures, you could easily add another two or three thousand people to the colony, but not under the threat of being second class citizens, useful only as a labor force."

"You're right, Captain. Dammit, how are we ever going to get past the resentments. There's a lot of people who still blame the former captain and crew for abandoning us on that planet anyway."

"And they are right to do so," said the former captain.

"Grandfather?"

"That was implicit in our sealed orders, the ones we opened after we originally set sail from Earth. We were to drop off our passengers then abandon them there forever, go back for another load to deliver to a different destination. People, the original plan was to seed mankind throughout the galaxy, in hopes that a few patches could manage to survive and thrive.

"Everyone knew Earth was doomed, the fools in power would destroy the planet for their own gain. This was the plan to make certain humanity survived. When we couldn't find a suitable planet for ourselves we decided to return to Elysium, hoping to join the colony there. You know how that worked out."

"Did you ever check in on any of the other groups?" asked Jeannie.

"No. You see, each captain was ordered to destroy any record of the location of the colony they left behind."

"But you didn't."

"No, I didn't. I suspected I had a granddaughter in that colony, and I secretly hoped to find a way back there. Once the crews were blended, I planned to find a planet for them, then build a small ship to come looking for Elysium.

"Forgive me, Jeannie, but I never quite believed your mother's story, and I hoped to find you as an adult woman, introduce myself, and hope we could have a DNA test to verify. When we failed to find a suitable planet, I took the senior staff into my confidence, and we agreed to come back."

"Well I for one, am damn glad you did," said Miriam. "At least some of us managed to survive because of that."

"Second that," muttered the man beside her. "So, what are we going to do here?"

The captain seemed to slip into thought and Amanda had to nudge her to bring her attention back to the room. "Sorry, people. All right, we have problems, more than you know. The SUVI have been getting a bad feeling about this planet. None of us can pinpoint what the issue might be, but several of us are growing steadily more uneasy about it.

"Rest assured, we will investigate this planet thoroughly before any attempt is made to settle people there. Moreover, Ship 87643 is being refitted with faster engines, so he can come find the Reacher if needs be. We are also refitting another of the Earalithian ships to carry passengers in case an evacuation is required."

"An evac to where? That ship would need a half-dozen or more trips to get three thousand people off planet."

"Relax, Miriam, I plan to find a suitable spot on the planet itself for a fall back position. Should the need arise, Ship could come for us while the other got everybody back to a safe waiting area."

Suvi-jean stopped speaking and gazed at the two representatives of the colonists. Slowly her eyes turned amber, and she rose from her chair to begin pacing about. "Unfortunately, the most sensible approach will find few, if any, interested in pursuing it."

"Jeannie?"

"Grandfather, as it stands now there are actually too few people to make a viable colony, but no one will acknowledge that. The wisest course of action would be to remain on the Reacher until the population increases to ship's capacity, and then establish a colony.

"Right now, as has already been noted, the true colonists are getting too old for this, there are too few young among them to take over the task, and we still have issues to work through. In a few generations the population will grow, and the differences should vanish. That would be the appropriate time to establish a colony."

"I have to agree with you on this one, Jeannie," sighed Eamon Reilly, "but you'll have the devil's own time trying to sell it to the gr ... sorry, passengers."

"By everything you hold holy, people, is there not a single human willing to work toward the greater good of the group?"

"Easy, Captain, easy," grinned Jake. "I know we're a hard-headed species. It'll take you a few generations to get us fully trained."

Slowly she reached for Amanda's hand and chuckled. "All right, big brother, I'm wide open to suggestions here."

"I suggest we do as planned, check out this planet, make damn sure it isn't going to go crazy on us, then re-visit the conversation. Right now we're all getting worked up over speculation. Who knows, the planet could be a paradise, or another barren mistake. Why not reserve judgement until we get a look at the place."

"He's right," agreed Miriam. "If the SUVI are getting bad vibes about the place, it may be we'll have to bypass it anyway. There's no rush, is there? If the planet proves good, the ship could hang around for a year or two before you run off to play, couldn't it?"

Suvi-jean nodded her head and her eyes began to return to normal. "Yes, that does make sense. A year or more should tell us if it's safe to leave and go exploring, or not.

"So, we're agreed the best course of action is to investigate first. If it looks good, then we establish the colony and allow it to take root before we set out to explore." There was a round of nodded agreement at that. "Then we have a plan of action. Commander Jones, what's our estimated time of arrival?"

"Another six days should put us in orbit around the planet, Captain. We've found several artificial satellites in orbit there, but nothing active. I suspect most of it has been there a long time."

"Well then, we have six days to solve all the problems. Let's make wise use of that time we have left."

With that the meeting broke up. Suvi-jean took Amanda's hand and led her back to their quarters. "Jeannie, you're still bugged. What is it? What's nagging at you?"

"Sweet Mandy, promise me you'll be careful."

"Of course. Jeannie?"

"It's the damned planet, Mandy. I have this terrible sense it will try to take you away from me."

Amanda searched her eyes for several moments, then spoke. "I'll be extra careful, I promise."

Chapter 16

First Look

The #3 mess was abuzz with raised voices as Miriam Holbrooke delivered her report. "Bypass the planet, but what are we supposed to do? Dammit, we're not getting any younger ..."

Miriam raised her hand for silence. "I know, I know, and I agree with you here, but remember Elysium, remember how fast those Oraks hit us the first time. They appeared out of nowhere and took out half our numbers.

"People, I understand, I do. The problem is, we need to bring up our numbers, and half the Reacher's crew might be willing, but we haven't been all that welcoming. Those years in the caverns of Elysium were hard years. We were beaten down, controlled, and powerless, under the thumb of a mad dictator.

"Sadly, that had an effect on us, all of us. It made us distrustful where weren't before. Originally, we worked together, but in the caverns we learned distrust and greed. We learned to hoard resources rather than share."

She paused for a moment. "And look what it did to us. Instead of helping each other we turned on each other. We watched as dozens were sent to the surface to survive as best they could. None did.

"Now we face the possibility of establishing another colony with only the few hundred of us who remain. We could recruit another one or two thousand, but they're afraid of us, afraid they'll be marginalized, refused access to resources, be only accepted as a labor force, second class citizens. Here on the Reacher everyone can access the ships resources as needed. If we're to have a hope of recruiting the people we need we will have to assure them that will not change on the colony.

"You know this is true; a colony can only survive if everyone works together. We have to get past this, past the conditioning of the caverns."

The meeting went on well into the night with little resolved, and Miriam retired to her quarters with a heavy heart. The conditions in

165

the caverns had been harsh, and Farouk Bladon had kept them at each other's throats for over seventeen years. That mindset was going to be hard to overcome.

* * * * *

The next morning they were in the launch bay, the captain fussing, her instincts going on full alert. "Mandy ..."

"Jeannie honey, I've got this, and my bodyguard is on full alert, so is my security guy. We'll be careful, I promise."

"I know, please don't think I lack faith in your abilities, it's just that ..."

"You love me and you're being a mother hen?"

Suvi-jean sighed. "Yeah, that. All right, I'll stop. Go take a look at this one. You may launch when ready."

Amanda kissed her cheek then boarded Explorer. "Crew all here?"

"Crew here and ready, Commander." Amanda saw Thirteen dressed in his old hunting leathers, two wicked looking blades hanging on his belt. She raised an eyebrow at him and he grinned. "This gear is comfortable, what can I say?"

"You know a blaster has more range."

"That's Hal's job, those things scare me."

Amanda just shook her head and stepped to the co-pilot's chair. "Ready Three?"

"Ready, Commander, we already have clearance for launch."

"Take us out. Let's go have a look at this thing." Explorer slipped from the launch bay then shot down toward the planet far below. She moved into a low orbit and began her scans. "Morthel, anything moving?"

"Just the small ship beside us."

"Small ship ... is that Linsey's ship?"

"I believe it is, Commander."

"For the love of mercy." Muttering, Amanda reached for the comm. "Explorer to Ship 87643. Linsey, is that you playing at being my shadow?"

"Busted," came the laughing reply. "I've got my gunner here and Eighteen as well. Eighteen says something's amiss here, so we decided to ride shotgun on this one. My ship is armed and Mendalo is deadly on the guns."

"Ah-huh, can't talk you into going back?"

"Sorry Commander, but this is an alien planet, it's my job to check it out too."

"Jeannie put you up to this, right?"

"Commander Drake, this is Eighteen. The idea is mine, I'm afraid. Commander, please be extremely careful if you set foot on that planet."

Amanda sighed then responded. "Understood, Eighteen. All right let's all have a look at her. Three, begin standard search pattern."

"Beginning grid search, Commander."

"Hal, are you getting anything on your sensors?"

"Nothing's moving down there that I can see. Morthel?"

"I'm seeing lots of ruins, no life signs. Nothing but desert here." A while later they were flying over dense foliage. "There's plenty of plant growth here, lots of life signs, but no Earalithian life signs, just birds and animals, and more ruins. Are we going down, Commander?"

"Not yet. I want to check the whole planet first. We'll keep going."

In all Amanda took two whole days to explore from above before she chose a landing site. They'd found a lot of desert, some jungle, and a band of more temperate climate with forests of smaller trees covering most of it, beneath it all lay the ruins of a once thriving colony. They found lakes, rivers, islands large and small, but always only ruins.

There was only one place where they found what they thought were signs of less damage than everywhere else. It was on a large island with low mountains at the forested edge of a grassland that ran into a nearby desert then down to the sea. For some reason, the ruins here didn't appear as badly damaged.

On the third day they set the ship down in a large clearing near a small lake. Thirteen was first through the hatch with a heavily armed Hal White close behind. "Looks good to me, Thirteen?"

The lean man sniffed the air and gazed all around with those piercing eyes that missed nothing. "It looks clear, but I don't like it."

"Thirteen?" came the call from inside the ship.

"All right, Commander, come on out, but everybody stay alert."

Within moments Lilly Peters had men bringing out the storage crates for her as she avidly collected sample after sample of the plant life that abounded beside the lake. By the end of day, she had three of the huge crates full.

Through it all Thirteen and Hal patrolled the area, fully alert for danger. As darkness fell the ship rose to a low orbit while the crew rested and recuperated. "Morthel, you've been on those sensors all day, you get anything?"

"Plenty of animals and birds, Commander, but no signs of organized life forms. I'd really like to have a look through some of those ruins. We could learn much from what we might find there."

"I agree. Thirteen, what do you think? Is it safe for us to go poking around the old ruins?"

"If Mr. Sacumbtu is willing to have two of his men keep watch with Hal, I'll go with you."

"All right, we have a plan. Tomorrow we'll take a look at some of those ruins. Get some rest, people."

When dawn arrived on the surface the Explorer was already back on the ground. Thirteen took a hard look around before he gave the all-clear for the others to disembark. Nothing had been disturbed from the day before. This time Lilly kept her group out in the open near the water's edge while Amanda, Morthel, and Thirteen went into the ruined city.

The buildings were Earalithian in design, but most were partially broken down, the streets littered with rubble from falling walls, and everywhere plant life was trying to reclaim what had been wrested from the world so long ago.

They explored building after building no success. They found nothing of value and nothing to indicate what had happened to the people who had built this place. All in all, it had been quite disappointing. Once they were back in orbit, had consumed a meal, and were relaxing, Amanda reported in to Jeannie aboard the Reacher.

"No, sweetheart, absolutely nothing happened, we didn't find a living soul nor any real trace of what happened here. Lilly's uprooted half the planet and has it in storage, but she's the only one of us who've had any success. From what we can gather about the ruins, there are several layers of civilization, each built up on the ruins of the one before it."

"Okay, so far so good, but Mandy, I beg you, do not let down your guard. This isn't over yet."

* * * * *

The next morning on the planet began as the others, peacefully. Once again Amanda and Morthel set out with Thirteen in the lead. They went deeper into the ruins, working their way towards a taller building that seemed to have defied the ravages of time better than the rest.

As they neared it, Morthel declared it reminded her of the ancient temples on her home world. She was right, it appeared to be a temple, constructed of heavy material, designed to withstand the worst storms nature could throw at it. As they stood facing the wide doors, Morthel grinned and spoke. <Temple, open.>

With a groan of protest the aged doors shivered a few times then slowly pushed aside the rubble and swung open. "Let me," said Thirteen as he stepped in front of Amanda and led the way into the ancient building.

Inside they found a tight entryway that led to a cavernous room with row after row of seats facing forward towards what appeared to be some sort of altar. They were halfway there when Thirteen shouted the warning and pushed Amanda behind a fallen pillar. She was stunned at his speed as he dodged or batted aside number of armed robots that charged toward them.

Thirteen managed to get Morthel behind the sheltering pillar with Amanda, but he took a few injuries in the process.

Thirteen destroyed a dozen or more, but Commander Drake and Morthel were gone, and he could not follow them. Without hesitation he turned and threw himself at the machines blocking the door. It took all his strength and speed, but the last machine finally fell, granting him a path to freedom. He was already on the comm as he burst through the wide-open doorway to see the captain racing toward him.

* * * * *

Suvi-jean had been having breakfast with Jake when SUVI 20 came hurrying towards them, dragging Eamon Reilly by the hand. "Captain ..."

"Easy, Twenty, easy. Tell me what it is."

"Captain, I don't know how I know, but I just know things."

"Yes, Thirteen has said your intuition is remarkable, even for a SUVI. Tell me what it is and where."

"We're about to be under attack."

Before Jeannie could respond the entire ship lurched. "Battle stations, battle stations, Captain to the bridge. Emergency status red. Repeat, emergency status red."

The warning was still sounding as Jeannie came running onto the bridge with Jake, Twenty, and Eamon close behind. Before she could speak the ship lurched again. "Emmet, report."

"We're being attacked, Captain. Some sort of energy beam from the surface. Our new energy shield seems to be holding, but I have no idea for how long. Engines are down, navigation is down, and comms are down."

"Comms back up," called a voice from beneath a control panel.

"Captain to Engineering."

"Moira here. I'm a bit busy here."

"Report."

"Engines are down. We got hit without any warning, took out the engines. We got the energy shield up and it seems to be holding." The Reacher lurched again.

"How long?"

"How long for what? The engines to get us the hell out of here or how long before the shields fail, and we get blown to bits?"

"All of it."

"I'll need two days to repair the engines. The shields won't last that long."

"Is there a pattern to the attacks?"

"None that I can see. Captain, we can't take a lot more of this before we start coming apart."

"Understood, Captain out." Once again SUVI 20 was trying to get her attention. "Twenty, what is it?"

"On the surface, you need me with you, and we need to go armed. The source of the weapon is near where the Explorer landed. We can find it and knock it out."

SUVI-jean spun around. "Jake, arm heavy, bring more, and meet us at the transportation room." She was already talking to his disappearing form. "Twenty, can you tell me anything else, anything at all?"

"Commander Drake and Morthel are in danger, Thirteen will need medical attention. We need to go now. We have to shut down that energy beam."

"Come." Jeannie was already running toward the transportation room, Twenty close behind her. Eamon gave up the chase and got onto the comms with Carla down on the surface. Jake was already waiting in the transport room. He passed her a belt with two hand blasters attached.

"Tell me we can transport."

"Yes, Captain, we still have transportation," replied the young man at the controls.

"Then get us down there." They stepped onto the transport pad and vanished from the Reacher, reappearing near the temple ruins where their people had last been recorded by the ship's sensors.

"That way," said Twenty as she pointed then set out at a run. Jeannie sped past her just as Thirteen came through the doors reaching for his comms.

"Stay back from me. I have open wounds and my virus just went live. Stay back."

Jeannie skidded to a halt, her arm out straight to keep Jake back. "Thirteen, report."

"Robots, automated defense system is my guess. The temple appears to have tunnels beneath. They caught us in the open, the Commander and Morthel escaped while I fought them, but I lost track of them. I took a few wounds; one must have been poisonous and suddenly my virus went live to fight it.

"The poison has been neutralized, but I have open wounds and a live virus. Keep the humans back." He moved painfully aside to give Jeannie and her guards safe passage as Carla came racing towards them.

"Stay back, Carla, Thirteen's virus has gone live, and he has open wounds. You dare not get close."

"Understood. You go on, Jeannie, I've got this."

Suvi-jean nodded then led Twenty and Jake toward the open doors. Carla approached Thirteen cautiously. "Stay back, I'm live now, contagious, too dangerous. I need the berries if there are any left."

"Stay there and be still. You need those wounds bandaged. Just try to relax and let me work."

"It's too dangerous for you, Commander Marks. Stay back."

"All right, but you sit still and let me think." He started to grin and she shook a finger at him. "I know, I know, use my brain." She reached for her comm. "Carla to Lilly."

"Lilly here."

"Thirteen has been wounded and his virus is live. Please tell me you have more of those berries on the Reacher."

"Yes Ma'am we do. As long as we have SUVI I intend to keep a few bushes in production. I'll have my father transport them to your location as soon as possible."

A few moments later Eighteen appeared carrying a container of berries and a med kit. "I'm no medic, Commander, but I am immune to the virus. You stand back and give me directions; I'll do my best to put him back together."

Thirteen grinned as she handed him the berries and began to clean and bandage his wounds under Carla's direction. When she finished she accepted the empty container and stepped back. "Give it an hour or more, Commander, then you can check what I've done and proceed from there."

Carla saw Thirteen watching her and knew what he was thinking, what he wanted her to do. She fully agreed. "Eighteen, have you any medical training?"

"None at all."

"Would you be willing to learn some first aid from me?"

"For incidents like this when there's a live virus involved; you want me to be the official SUVI first aid person? You believe I have an aptitude for this?"

"I do. I saw you with Tara, SUVI 20, and just now. You're the right woman for the job."

With a shy smile, she nodded. "All right, Commander. Once you're back on the Reacher let me know when you have the time to teach me."

"Stay here. Once it is safe we'll do a lesson on Thirteen, use him for the practice dummy." Thirteen chuckled and shook his head as

Eighteen agreed. Now the captain just had to find the source of that weapon and shut it down.

* * * * *

Suvi-jean led them into the temple at a run. There were a number of destroyed robots scattered about. Thirteen's combat prowess was clearly exceptional. Standing amid the debris left behind by Thirteen, Suvi-jean cast about. "Any idea which way?"

"There, into that tunnel," replied Twenty as Jake passed her a strange looking weapon. "I have no idea how to use that."

"Point the skinny end at the baddies and pull that trigger. Never aim it at a friend, or any of the people on your team."

"Understood." She stepped in behind Jake as he followed Suvi-jean into the tunnel.

They didn't go far before the first robot appeared from the wall beside them. The small machine struck at Suvi-jean, but it was slow compared to a SUVI hunter and she tore the weaponized arm from its body then smashed it into the floor.

She didn't even pause as she stepped past the wreck to engage another. That machine fell to Jake's weapon before Suvi-jean could reach it.

The cavern opened up somewhat. Rubble was everywhere and signs of old buildings, or at least their foundations, were scattered about. The small machines were appearing from several open ports to rush at them. They soon lay shattered from the wrath of Suvi-jean.

The room exited into three different tunnels. "This way," said Twenty as she stepped toward one of the openings. A robot came flying right at her, but, reflexively, she caught it then used it to bat aside a few more before smashing it against the wall.

Jake stepped up beside her, swept a scatter blaster up to his shoulder, then pulled the trigger. There was a *whoosh* then a series of crashes from within the tunnel. He winked at Twenty as Suvi-jean went past them into the opening. They followed closely.

There were a number of twists and turns then Suvi-jean stepped on something that went *click*. She leaped aside as a huge, sharpened stake dropped from the roof and swung toward her. Twenty grabbed Jake by the jacket and pulled him aside as the large missile sped past then dropped to the floor with a dull thud.

Wide-eyed he gazed at the log that had nearly impaled him, then at Twenty. She winked at him then gently pushed him after Suvi-jean who was already moving again. Jake swallowed hard then nodded and followed his captain. He found her in another wide-open area, pinned down by a large number of robots. He ran past her firing the big blaster.

The attacking machines were hurled against the walls to lay shattered on the floor. "That way." Suvi-jean nodded and set out into the tunnel Twenty had indicated.

This new tunnel soon began to twist and turn as it sloped steeply downward. At one point, Suvi-jean stooped and swept up a shiny object. "Jeannie, what was that?" asked Jake.

"Amanda's locket. I've already retrieved her ring and rank insignia. She trying to leave us a trail."

"That means she's still alive. We'll find her, little sister, we'll find her."

The tunnel leveled off a bit, turned and climbed upwards, then opened up to another space with several more tunnels leading away. Again, this place was guarded. A metal arrow ripped through Jake's sleeve, and, with a muttered oath, he swept up his weapon and fired. There was a clank, then a robot toppled over a high ledge and fell to shatter on the floor below. "Take that, ya little fucker."

"Come on," said Suvi-jean as she led them through a zig-zag pattern towards the far wall.

"Third tunnel on the left, Captain." Jeannie nodded and changed direction. This tunnel was also protected, and more machines poured in behind them. Jake stepped past Jeannie and opened fire with the big blaster, clearing the path forward. As he did, Twenty opened fire behind them with the weapon Jake had given her. He chuckled at her "Wow, that worked well."

The next tunnel continued down, but it was different this time, some of the flooring was paved, and the ceilings were higher. They came to a room that had metal walls, paved floors, and cooling fans working. It opened up into a much larger space.

"There, that way." Suvi-jean leaped away in the direction Twenty had pointed.

"Dammit," muttered Jake as he gave chase.

"Come on, keep up," chided Twenty as she sped past him. She grinned as she heard his mutter reply.

He caught them at the beginnings of a steep ramp. "Stop fooling around, both of you. I can't protect you if you keep running away from me."

"Sorry," replied Twenty, but she was grinning.

"The hell you are. So now what? We going down?"

"We are, but I don't think we'll face a lot more opposition," replied Twenty.

"Somehow that doesn't reassure me," muttered Jake as he followed Suvi-jean out onto the downward spiraling ramp.

The ramp led downward to another room with a mix of machinery and paved pathways. "Follow the dark pathway." Suvi-jean nodded and set out, moving swiftly. A moment later Jake started to swear as a panel opened and another sort of mechanical robot came out. As it advanced it reached towards Jeannie, but Jake's blaster blew it against the wall, shattering it into a dozen pieces.

They encountered three more before they found the huge doorway with two figures beside it. "Jeannie!" Amanda flew into her lover's arms, as Suvi-jean hugged her tightly, cooing soothing sounds and kissing her hair.

"Oh my sweet Mandy, are you hurt?"

"No love, I'm not hurt. Morthel and I made our way down here to escape the robots. Every time we tried to go back the machines blocked our path. They kept saying, "Go back, safety lies below." Several came at us, but Morthel was able to warn them away. We tried to call for help, but the comms don't work down here.

"It's a suppressor field from my time," sighed Morthel. "All the temples used them, so the people were forced to pay attention. I've tried to shut it off, but no luck. It must be operated from inside."

"We can shut it down when we get inside."

"Sorry, Captain, but I can't get the doors to open."

"Well bugger," growled Jake. "Looks like we'll have to fight our way in. We've got to get inside and shut that damn thing down."

I have tried to get this door to open, but nothing I say will make this one budge."

"So it's busted?"

"No, Jake, I think I just haven't hit on the right phrase. I've tried all the usual commands and a number of other possibilities, but so far no luck. Why do you say we have to get inside?"

"The Reacher is under attack from an energy weapon. We've got to shut it down. My meter here says there's a big energy source behind that door. I'm betting this is the source of the attack."

"You could be right," replied Morthel. "It sounds like a planetary defense system got activated when I opened the temple doors. Okay, I'll try again because there is no way in the galaxy you could shoot your way past that door."

"Planetary defense system, Morthel?"

"I don't know for sure, Twenty. We know Earalith colonized here. I recall some of the people on our colony talking about building such a system in case the Empire found us."

"Maybe it is," said Suvi-jean. "Try a command with every word you can think of. We've got to get past that door."

Morthel nodded, turned back to the huge doors, and began. Several long tense moments later she hit it. <Archives, open.> With a groan of protest, the mighty doors shivered then slowly began to swing inward.

Cautiously, Suvi-jean led them inside. Morthel stepped to an open space and spoke in a clear ringing voice. <Archives, awaken.> Lights came up and a voice spoke from the walls in Earalithian.

<Greetings, exalted of Earalith. What do you seek?>

<Disengage defense system.>

<Defense system disengaged. What do you seek?>

<We seek knowledge of this place.>

"Morthel, the suppressor field?"

"Of course, Captain." <Suppressor field, disengage.> "Try your comms now, Captain."

She nodded her thanks. "Captain Sorenson to the Reacher, Reacher acknowledge."

* * * * *

The Reacher rocked under yet another blow from the energy beam. "We've lost our stabilizers, Commander. Orbit starting to decay."

"Dammit. Bridge to Engineering."

"Engineering here."

"We've lost our stabilizers, orbit is decaying."

"I'm aware of that," growled Moira Duncan as she worked feverishly. "I need time to get this fixed, time without the ship constantly shuddering and shaking my hands."

"Right now you've got less than one hour before we crash into that planet, Chief Engineer. You might want to step it up a bit. Bridge out."

"Step it up, he says. How about holding the bloody ship steady for a few minutes while I ... ah, there, that's got it. Got the shields back up. Now for the stabilizers."

Once again the ship rocked. "Orbit decaying faster, Commander."

"Understood. Engin ..."

"Sir, I've got comms from the surface, it's the captain."

"Bridge here, Captain. Have you had any success?"

"We've shut down the weapon, Emmet, do I still have a ship to come back to?"

"You will if Engineering can effect a few quick repairs, but we're not in great shape at the moment."

"Stabilizers back on line, orbit re-established."

"Captain, it appears that you'll have a ship to come home to after all."

"That is good news, Emmet. Patch me through to Engineering now." Commander Jones made a gesture with his hand and the comms officer flipped a switch.

"Engineering here. If you want the damn ship repaired, get off the bloody comms and let me work."

"Sorry, Moira, but I need your Earalithian engineer down here."

"Jeannie? Did you get the damned weapon shut off?"

"We did, but I want the blasted thing dismantled."

"I'll send him down with a crew as soon as I get Reacher tidied up."

"Sounds good. Sorenson out."

"Captain to the Reacher."

"Commander Jones aboard the Reacher responding. Captain, do you need assistance?"

"We do. I need six heavily armed security people and Commander da Silva down here if the transporters can reach us."

"One moment, Captain. Yes, the transporters can reach you."

"Send them down as soon as you can. I'll set a marker at the door."

She stepped outside the door and laid her comm button on the ground. A moment later six armed troops and Linsey appeared. "Keep an eye on those tunnels, nothing's come out of them since we got here, but watch them anyway. If hostile robots appear, deal with it. Linsey, this way."

"Wow!" Linsey was obviously impressed as Suvi-jean led her inside. "What is this place?"

"Apparently, the Earalith built a temple on the surface, but also established archives and defense systems deep underground for some reason. This one is all your baby now; I'm taking Commander Drake back to the Reacher."

"I have my own ship to go back to," said Amanda. "Morthel and I need to get back and reassure our people we're all right. Did Thirteen make it out?"

"He left a couple dozen shattered robots behind him, but he made it out," grinned Jake.

"All right then, call Explorer and see if her transporters can get us topside."

"Aye, Captain," grinned Amanda as she reached for her comm. A few moments later she and the captain plus Morthel, Jake, and SUVI 20 were standing in the sun beside the Explorer.

"Mandy, dear heart, are you certain you're all right?"

"I am. I'll admit I was scared to death, and had a minor meltdown when you rescued me, but I'm okay now."

"All right, if you're sure. Go see to your people, but bring the ship home for a twenty-four rest period for your crew before you do any more exploring."

Amanda grinned and gave her arm a gentle squeeze. "Yes, Mom."

Jeannie smiled then stepped back and called for a transport back to the Reacher for herself and SUVI 20. As they appeared in the transport room Jeannie turned to Twenty. "SUVI 20, I owe you more than I can say. I ..."

"No, Captain, I was sick and in pain, you held me, told me we're sisters, and so we are, SUVI sisters. There's no debt between us, ever."

"Thank you. So, you're getting used to being an alien?"

She was grinning and Twenty laughed with delight. "I had no real idea, but I'm slowly learning just how different we are. We are indeed alien, but the more I discover about this, the more intrigued I am by it all."

"That is good news. I'm so pleased for you. I have to check on the ship now, but how about joining me at the captain's table for dinner."

"Love to." She smiled as the captain walked away and Jake appeared on the transport pad. "Hi Jake, you okay?"

"Huh? What? Sure I am. Why do you ask?"

"Well, you went to war with the SUVI today, even managed to keep up for the most part. Not bad for a human."

"Not bad for a human? Really? You have no idea what hard work it is babysitting a couple of wild SUVI. I'll need to sleep for a week."

She just chuckled and walked away. Puzzled he turned to the woman at the transport controls. "Correct me if I'm wrong, but did she just flirt with me?"

"Ah-huh, that she did. She's a SUVI, she's already married, and so are you. You could be in a whole heap of trouble."

"Oh boy." He swallowed hard and walked away, returning to the Security office.

Chapter 17

A Glimpse of the Past

Antha joined Linsey and Eighteen in the cavern of the archives. "Commander Linsey, how can I assist? What is this place?"

"We believe it's some sort of archive of the colony that was here as well as a defense system placement. I asked you to come down as we may need you to open a few doors, things like that."

"But Linsey, you and Eighteen both speak Earalith as well as I do now."

"Yes, but you're from that culture, we're not. There will be technologies we don't understand, aren't aware of, won't know how to activate, things like that."

"I understand. I confess, I too would love to discover the ultimate fate of the colony, what became of those people so long ago. Where do we begin?"

"I have no real idea; you take the lead on this one."

"As you wish. I see Dorind and friends are already hard at work. May I ask what they're doing?"

"They're dismantling the weapon system that attacked the Reacher. The captain isn't taking any chances it might go active again."

Antha grinned at that. "Can't blame her for that."

Linsey laughed. "As for us, first we have to learn what we can down here for the captain. I'm a bit surprised Morthel didn't access the place for her."

"My most cherished would not know how, Commander Linsey. She is of the noble class. To gain information from a place like this she would have sent someone of the lower classes, like me. Now, let's see what we can do." <Archive, voice search.>

<Authorization.>

<Antha, third colonization wave, servant of Lady Morthel.>

<Access granted. Search parameters?>

<Bring to me the histories of this colony from the beginning to the present.>

<Working. Approach visual display panel.>

Antha spent several hours building a coherent history of the fall of the colony. While she gathered and studied information, Linsey and Eighteen spent their time poking around the items set out on display.

Antha looked up as they entered the room where she was working. She removed the head piece she was wearing and set it aside along with her recording device. Slowly rising from the seat, she sighed deeply. "My friends, it's a sad business to read about your contemporaries as ancient history."

Linsey nodded and smiled warmly at her. "How much more do you have to do?"

"I believe I can stop now. It'll take me a while to compile this into a report for you to take to the captain. The short version is the Empire found them; found and eliminated them. They'd built this defense system for just such an emergency, but it failed to protect them.

"Obviously the Empire ships avoided it. When Morthel opened the doors above she must have triggered it."

Eighteen smiled warmly as Linsey gathered Antha into her arms and held her gently. "Let it go, Antha. We're your people now, the people on the Reacher, and we're safe now. We, all of us, are the endings of an older race, and yet, we're the beginnings of a new and vital people."

Antha hugged Linsey tighter for a moment then released her, stepping back shyly. "Thank you for that, Linsey. I did need it. What do you need me to do now?"

"Take what you have back to the Reacher, report to Captain Sorenson, then talk to the rest of the Earalith. They'll want to know what you've learned."

Antha nodded then stepped to the middle of the room, calling for transport. She vanished in a flash of light. "Now what?" asked Eighteen.

"Now we go," sighed Linsey. "We close it up and go, it's not ours and it's not salvage. All we have the right to take from here is information."

They walked outside then Linsey closed the archives. <Archive, return to state of rest. Close.>

<Archive closing.> The huge doors swung closed and Eighteen called for transport. They returned to the office, a strange sense of sadness falling on them.

* * * * *

While Linsey and Eighteen were closing up the archives, another door was also closing on the past. Dr. Eamon Reilly sat having a drink with his friend and former captain, Olga Volkov. "All right, Eamon, out with it. You look like you've just lost your best friend."

"I have."

"Eamon?"

"It's Tara, SUVI 20 I guess she is now. I didn't really understand, had no idea what I'd done by injecting her with that virus."

"I thought you two were giving it another try."

"We did, but I released her, Olga. In truth I guess my Tara died thirty years ago. All this time I've just been chasing a dream, a memory. Oh yes, there's still parts of Tara in her, but she so different now, and changing almost daily, growing in her abilities.

"Oh hell, even if I'd managed to succeed as I'd hoped, even if I'd restored Tara to what she was before, she'd still be thirty years younger. It never could have worked; I can see that now."

"So you set her free?"

"Yes."

"And now?"

"And now what?"

"And now what will you do? You've still got a lot of good years in you, Eamon, and a wealth of talent and knowledge. What will you do with that?"

"I have no idea at all. Any suggestions?"

"You spent thirty years working towards a single goal, and for good or ill, SUVI 20 is the result of that, your child, if you will. The SUVI are different, but I'm sure there's a lot you can learn then pass on about their uniqueness."

Eamon Reilly chuckled at that. "Figure out the SUVI? Now that sure would be a challenge." She smiled to see the sparkle return to his eye. "Make sure my Frankenstein's monster has a long and healthy life?"

"Ah-huh."

"Sure, why not. I guess if she has any offspring they will be technically my grandchildren. All right, I'll accept that challenge."

"Now you're talking. One more for the road?"

"Aye, one more for the road."

* * * * *

While Olga and Eamon shared one for the road, the Captain sat quietly listening to Antha's report. When she finished Jeannie gave her a gentle smile and patted her hand. "Be at peace, Antha, you've done well. That was a fine piece of work, and a clear and concise report. You're a true asset to the Reacher. I'm also aware of the counselling work you've been doing. I'm pleased you've taken on this role. Thank you."

With a shy smile of appreciation, Antha left the captain's briefing room.

Chapter 18

Taking a Hard Look

"Have all ships returned, Emmet?"

"Aye, Captain, all ships have returned and reported in."

"Are all repairs on the Reacher complete?"

"They are, Captain. It's actually a good thing that Recovery ran into that bit of trouble. That prompted us to get more shielding and that saved the ship. Without it we'd have been finished. Reacher is now ship-shape and good as new, better than ever in fact."

"Explain."

"Engineering recovered the weapon that attacked us. They've mounted it on the Reacher as a defensive weapon. We call it the energy cannon."

Jeannie chuckled at that. "Very good, now it's time to put our heads together and decide what to do next. Call a meeting of the senior staff and the passenger's representatives."

"Aye, Captain." She turned and strode from the bridge toward the briefing room to the sound of the call over the speaker system. "All senior staff to the bridge. Repeat, all senior staff to the bridge. Passenger representatives to the bridge briefing room. Repeat, passenger representatives to the bridge briefing room."

Jeannie paced as she waited for them all to arrive. "Looks like we're all here, Captain."

She took her place and leaned her elbows on the table. "Thank you, Brandon. All right people, all ships have returned. It's time to take a hard look at the possibilities of this planet. Let's start with the finding of the first contact. Commander Drake, report."

Amanda smiled and winked at her. "Aye, Captain Sorenson. The Explorer, in the company of Ship 87643, spent two full days doing an aerial inspection of the planet. We found a variety of climate conditions from deserts to jungles, lakes, rivers, and oceans.

"We also observed abandoned colonies, but we saw no sign of active civilization, so we landed at the most likely spot and began to explore more closely. Unfortunately, we triggered an ancient planetary defense system.

"We also discovered an ancient archive that was still functioning. From it we learned that the original colonists had been attacked by Earalith Empire and is no more."

As Amanda stopped speaking, Jeannie gave her hand a gentle squeeze. "Thank you, Commander. You have a botanist on your ship's crew, do we have a report from her?"

"Shall I call her in?"

"Please do."

Amanda reached for her comm. "Ensign Lilly Peters to the bridge briefing room."

"On my way, Commander." A few moments later she arrived.

"Sub-Commander Peters, can you give us your opinion of the planet below."

"My opinion ... wait, did you just promote me?"

"Yes I did."

"Wow, thank you Captain Sorenson. Yes, the planet. I took a number of samples of the plant life found there, plus a number of soil samples from a variety of locations. I haven't had much time to study them, but I do have some preliminary findings. Captain, the plant life appears to be struggling for nutrients which explains the slow advance of the deserts."

"Your recommendations?"

"It could be done, Captain. It'll take a lot of work and a long time, but a colony could survive there, bring back the soil surrounding the colony, but it'll be a hard road and a long one. Eventually the population would probably outpace the rate of soil recovery. On a scale of one to ten I'd give this one a four at best."

"I'm curious, Lilly," said Miriam Holbrooke. "What would you consider a ten?"

"A ten would be a young world, never seen an advanced civilization, never endured an early industrial age, rich in plant and animal life," she replied.

Jeannie smiled as she leaned her elbows on the table once again. "Lilly, why pre-industrial?"

"The early industrial age is a learning experience, Captain. The lands get ravaged, the air polluted, the water poisoned, etc. We as a people have already been through this and we've developed cleaner technologies, have a far greater understanding of the side effects of industry. Hopefully we could avoid messing up the planet as we grew in population."

"You mean, create a paradise of nature in harmony with industry and development?"

"Exactly, Captain, at least that is my hope, the dream for our species if you will."

"I like that dream, Lilly, thank you. All right, that the goods from Explorer. Recovery, report."

"Recovery has little to add, Captain," said Olga Volkov. "We went down for a look once Explorer gave the all-clear, but we actually found little that might be useful. We gave it up and came home."

"Recommendations?"

"Sub-commander Peters says it could be done, but I wouldn't want to try it."

"Fair enough. Thank you, Olga. Now for me. Speaking for the SUVI, a few of us have been down to the planet, conferred with the rest, and our collective vote is no. Should the passengers decide to try, the SUVI will not join you."

"I don't believe that'll become an issue, Captain." Miriam sighed and looked at the two men who accompanied her. They shook their heads no. "We will be recommending the colonists pass this one by.

Elysium took the good out of us, and we're in no hurry to take on another unknown. We'll have to take it back to the people, but I doubt there'll be a problem. If anyone makes a fuss, we'll remind them of the hostilities in the tunnels of Elysium when resources were limited."

Jeannie chuckled at that. "All right, that brings us down to the hard choice."

"The hard choice? You mean the prisoners?"

"Yes, Eamon, that's who I mean. Lilly, your opinion, could they survive on that planet?"

"Me? Oh, yes, let me see? There's plenty of shelter in the ruins, they could scavenge enough raw food to sustain themselves until they could grow more, the climate where Commander Drake encountered the defense system is mild enough, so, yes, I believe they could survive."

"Compared to the caverns on Elysium, this place looks good. All right, people, opinions, suggestions, recommendations?"

"You'd just dump them down there?"

Jeannie pulled the scarf away from her neck to show the now healed burn scars. "What would you have me do, Eamon? This is just a small reminder of their latest attack on me. How much compassion should I show them, how many more chances should I give them to bring harm to the population?"

He sighed deeply and sat back. "You're right, Captain. I apologize. I spoke out of turn and in error. Those men have had too many chances already. I'll start waking them up if you want to send them down to the surface."

"Thank you, Eamon. Anybody else? First officer?"

"Send them down, Captain. Send them down and be rid of them."

"Chief of Security?"

"Send them down to serve their sentence of exile, Captain. They've been through due process."

"Anybody else?" No one spoke. "Miriam?"

Miriam Holbrooke sighed and let her shoulders slump. "Send them down, Captain. Get this done so we can move on from all that. You know, before we were dropped on Elysium, many of those men had given no hint of their violent tendencies. Farouk Bladon encouraged that, fighting among ourselves. He saw it as allowing the strong to survive to make the species stronger. God, I hated that man.

"Send them down, Captain Sorenson, close that black chapter of all our lives."

"So be it, start waking them up, Eamon. Sheila, have your men on hand. As soon as one is awake, escort him to transportation and ship him out. We'll send down a few essential supplies once they're all on the surface."

The meeting broke up then, and Jeannie and Amanda soon found themselves alone in the briefing room. "Jeannie?"

"Hmmm?"

"What's bugging you, my sweet SUVI?"

"Oh, nothing and everything. You know, lots of people probably thought I had it all, the happy ending. I'd gone from slave to captain of the Reacher in less than a year. Plus I got the most amazing woman as companion. Happy ending, right? Everything anybody could ever want, right?"

"Not a happy ending for you, Jeannie?"

"Oh Mandy, don't doubt for a second that I'm happy, especially with you at my side. It's just that it's not the end, is it? It never ends. There's always a dozen or more things going on at once and I have to keep track of it all. Anybody who thinks the captain's job is easy is badly mistaken.

"Since I took this job I've had to send you away from me for weeks at a time, I've sent you into danger, and ..."

"Whoa, whoa, easy my love." Amanda gently pulled Jeannie into her arms and held her, cooing soothing sounds. "Sweet Jeannie, you're overwhelmed here, and I do understand that. I know how hard you work, and why. I'd be shocked if you didn't get overwhelmed once in a while, but that's what I'm here for, to hug you when it gets too heavy.

"You're a perfectionist, my lover, but nothing's ever perfect all the time. Jeannie, you've made changes to the command structure, promoted the people you trust to get the jobs done. Ease back a bit and let them work now, let them help you carry the load."

"How do you do it, Mandy?"

"Do what?"

"You're always so strong, in control, always so calm, never upset or flustered; how do you do it?"

"Oh, I'm a mess of self-doubt half the time, I just don't let anybody see it, I can't."

"Why not?"

"Because I'm companion to Suvi-jean Sorenson, super SUVI captain of the Reacher. Jeannie, everybody needs somebody to lean on from time to time. That's a big part of my job as your companion."

"You're working at being strong enough for me to lean on when I start to unravel. Mandy, I do lean on you, need you to keep me focused, on track. You have no idea how much I've come to depend on you, or do you? Thirteen's been coaching you, hasn't he?"

Amanda smiled and hugged her tighter for a moment. "Yes he has."

"Mandy, I don't want you to burn out, you need somebody to lean on too."

"I have you for that, my sweet Suvi-jean."

"Do you ever get overwhelmed?"

"Oh yeah, I do."

"But you've never said anything, ever. Mandy, I want to be there for you too."

"And you are, but my job as Captain's companion requires me to keep my own emotional issues very private. I talk to you when we're alone, and when I don't want to add to the load you carry, I talk to Antha."

"Beautiful companion of mine, you're a most amazing woman."

"Oh yeah? Tell me how amazing I am."

"How about I take you back to quarters and show you?"

Amanda laughed with delight to see the blue mood lift from her lover. "Delightful idea, sweetheart, take me away."

* * * * *

While the captain and Amanda slipped away for a few moments of afternoon delight, the first man was reviving in the cryo bay. He groaned and sat up. "Gods I'm cold. What the hell's going on ...?"

"Do you remember why you're here," asked Jake as he hauled the man to his feet.

The man blinked a few times as he shook off the last of the cryo headache. "Yes."

"Good. Now it's time to begin serving your sentence. You're going down to the surface forever. You can survive there, but it won't be easy."

"Hey, what about my trial? I didn't get a trial."

"You want a trial? Okay, here's how it works. Right now, you're facing exile. If you go to trial you'll be charged with mutiny. You attacked the captain and tried to take over the ship, that's mutiny. The penalty for mutiny, if found guilty, is death.

"So, still want the trial, or will you accept the exile?"

Grudgingly the man replied. "Exile."

"Smart man. Get moving." As Jake led him away to the transport room, Eamon Reilly began awakening another.

While Eamon continued to awaken the men sentenced to exile, and Jake escorted them to transport, the kitchen staff was busy preparing supplies for them. Each man would get a week's worth of rations, a few simple farming tools, some seeds, and a change of clothes. The rest was up to them.

They were dropped near the small lake where there was fresh water, shelter in the ruins of the old temple. The entire process took three days, but it was eventually finished, and Suvi-jean gave a sigh of relief when she got the report.

A short time later Miriam Holbrooke contacted the Captain to let her know the colonists had officially voted to pass this planet by and look for a better choice. Jeannie thanked her then headed for the bridge. "Captain on the bridge."

"As you were, people. Commander Jones, it looks like we're clear to go. We'll have to decide on a target, but that shouldn't take long."

"Actually, Captain, I'd like to stick around for a few more days."

"Oh? Talk to me, Emmet."

"We're at about half for fuel, Captain. That star seems to be building up for a flare or two. We could back off a bit out of harm's way, but we could use that flare to top up all our solar fuel cells."

"As could Explorer and Recovery, Ship as well. All right, Emmet, tuck her in where you want her and I'll go gather the clan so we can decide on our next target. You have the bridge."

As Jeannie left the bridge she got a call from Miriam Holbrooke. "Holbrooke to the Captain."

"You sound upset, Miriam, what's up?"

"Forgive me, Captain, but can you spare some time to speak to a gathering of the colonists?"

"Where?"

"Auditorium number three?"

"On my way." As she walked Jeannie called for Jake and a detail of security people.

"This is a mistake," growled Jake as he joined her in the corridors and learned what was about to happen.

"Yeah, could be, but it has to happen just this once. Call who you need to assist you, but we're doing this."

"On it."

Jeannie arrived at the auditorium in short order with Jake and a detail of well-armed security people. Security stood back out of the way as Jeannie took the stage and approached the microphone, but they stayed between her and the mass of people crowded into the room. "Greetings, passengers, elected officers, how can I be of service today?"

One man strode up to the floor mike. "I see you brought your goons with you, Captain."

"Forgive me, my friend, but no SUVI will walk into an auditorium full of Elysium's colonists without an armed escort, including me. As you may or may not know, I was recently attacked and put in a pain collar by members of your group. I'll do my best for you, and have tried to demonstrate that, but if you want my trust, you'll have to earn it.

"Now, before I open the discussions to the floor, I will speak with your elected officials. Miriam Holbrooke, as the elected president of this group, will you tell me why I've been summoned here?"

"Forgive me, Captain. A large number of our people are demanding clarification of a few things." She gave the Captain a sly wink.

Jeannie gave Miriam the slightest nod to say she understood. "I see. Very well, which points appear to be vague?"

At this point the man on the floor interrupted again. "We want to know what the status of our colony is, what efforts are being made to establish a new colony, what ..."

He got no further as Jeannie interrupted him. "I understand. I'll explain it so you can all understand the situation you find yourselves in. You are currently passengers on the Reacher. You are the refugees from a failed colony on Elysium. Your leaders tried to capture this ship and were defeated, yet you were brought aboard at your own request. You have no rights here, you have no status, and you will not summon me like this again.

"Moreover, I don't like or want you, and I have good reasons for this, yet I have agreed to take your situation and concerns under advisement, I asked for you all to elect officials to consult with me on a regular basis, and I have included these representatives in several staff meetings so they could keep all of you fully informed of what we're doing and why. I have also listened to their concerns, heard their advice, and I tell you now, that's as far as I will go.

"I'm SUVI, and I'm now captain of this ship which rescued you against my advice. The former captain of this ship brought you up from Elysium, and now we're trying to find a way through the mess we find ourselves in.

"The Reacher is under no compulsion or command to find you another planet to colonize, but we will try. However, I promise you, if you continue to make this difficult for me, I'll put you all off on the planet below then go about my business.

"So, are you all clear on your status now? You are passengers on this ship, and as far as I'm concerned, unwelcome passengers, a drain on ship's resources, a workload I advised the previous captain to avoid. I suggest you all put some thought into how you can make this easier for me, not harder.

"Is there anything further?"

There was only silence from the vast room. The large man had retreated, and no one seemed in a hurry to step up. "All right then, I will assume I have managed to make this clear for you. Now, if you'll all excuse me, I have work to do."

She reached for her comm. "All senior staff to the briefing room, repeat, all senior staff to the briefing room." She let her hand fall away from her shoulder. "Passenger representatives are invited to attend this meeting." They rose from their chairs and followed her out of the auditorium.

*****

"All requested personnel present, Captain."

"Thank you, First Officer. Miriam, what do you think, did I overdo it?"

That brought a great laugh from Miriam and her two companions. "No, Captain, you didn't overdo it, but you did get your point across. I think things will be a bit quieter from now on."

"Gods, I hope so," sighed Jeannie as she fairly melted back into her chair. "I swear, the next time one of them comes at me demanding ..."

"Easy, Captain, easy," chuckled Amanda as she patted Jeannie's hand. "I heard you'd gone to speak to all the passengers. I was halfway there when I got the announcement for this meeting. Can you tell us what happened?"

"I can tell you," grinned John Atwood, one of the passenger representatives. "Better yet I can show you." He pushed a com/cam across the table.

Amanda reached for it and placed it in a slot on the table. "Computer, full display." They all sat back and watched as Jeannie explained to the passengers exactly what their status was.

Brandon Hoffman was chuckling. "I think that was pretty clear, Captain."

"I like it," grinned Sheila Singh.

"Precise and very clear, Captain," smiled Olga Volkov. "There's no room for misinterpretation there."

"All right, let's hope that we've settled the passengers down and all is well there. Now for the next step. Emmet wants to hang around here for a few days to soak up a solar flare or two to top up our fuel. Once that's done, we can head out."

"Where to next, Captain?"

"I have no idea at all, Olga. None. In the archives, Antha learned the old empire is gone, as are two more that followed it. The Earalith from this planet abandoned it even as our people abandoned Earth. They too are out there searching for a new home. The point being, continuing to back track them seems a bit pointless now."

Everyone was silent for a while, then Jeannie spotted the grin on Eamon's face. "What is it Eamon?"

"Huh? Oh nothing."

"No, you had a thought. Let's hear it."

"I was just thinking about what you once said."

"Oh?"

"Yes. You said we should remain on the ship until our population reached full capacity, and only then consider establishing a colony. That makes sense to me, and I believe we could speed up that process a bit."

"What do you mean, speed up the process?"

"Well, as you may or may not know, each colony carried with it a bank of fertilized embryos, frozen, but ready to help populate the colony as needed and to help increase the gene pool."

"Yes but that was destroyed by the Oraks," said Miriam. "The storage facility was utterly destroyed."

"Not quite. We've had little time to explore everything brought up by the salvage crews from the ruined settlements. A few days ago SUVI 20 guided me to a crate which contained, in her words, a number of potential humans. It was a storage unit, still functioning, and containing a hundred embryos.

"I could thaw them out and start the process."

Jeannie leaned forward, her eyes focused on his. "Explain what you mean by starting the process."

"Yes, well, I start warming up the embryo, then either nurture it in the lab while it grows and develops, or it can be implanted into a woman who would then carry it to term."

"You're saying we'd need a hundred volunteer mothers?"

"Yes."

"Well, I suppose that should be possible considering our current population, plus the additional expansion of the gene pool would be a blessing. It certainly is something to consider."

"So, shall I start warming them up?"

Jeannie chuckled. "Not just yet. Let's think this one through a bit. However, I do like the idea of keeping everybody on the ship. This is a safe and controlled environment. If we're to nurture the human species back to health, perhaps we should be looking more for planets that will render up useful resources more than a planet to colonize.

"Yes, if we encounter a paradise for humans, then by all means, colonize it, but if not, stay safe while we grow in numbers. Give me your thoughts on this, people."

"I'm with you, Captain," sighed Miriam Holbrooke. "Elysium broke me, I'm over sixty now and in no hurry at all to run that risk again. Let's be a lot more cautious this time."

"I agree," said John Atwood, the second grounder representative. "Better to be safe than sorry. I'll back your idea." Everyone else agreed as well.

"Thank you all. So that's our plan, rest and grow strong again. Carla, how long can we last?"

"Me? Oh, well, forever I guess. We can make most of our own medicines if we can get the raw materials, and Hydroponics can supply much of that."

"Brandon?"

"Well, as long as we can gather a few resources we should be good for several generations."

Jeannie nodded. "Engineering?"

Moira Duncan chuckled. "Aye, Captain, we can keep the ships afloat for generations if we can mine a few planets for minerals, or salvage more of the Earalith tech. I say we're good to go."

"All right, we're in agreement and I'm pleased with that. Now all we have to decide is where to go next. Any thoughts?"

"Captain's prerogative," grinned Brandon Hoffman.

"Very well then. Commander Jones."

"Captain?"

"Once we've topped up our fuel, aim us at the nearest star system. We'll proceed in short hops, exploring and gathering as we go. So, inform your crews, your departments, your people, and get ready to move out."

* * * * *

Eighteen lay with her head pillowed on Linsey's shoulder. "Eighteen honey."

"Mmm?"

"You didn't seem too surprised to learn we'd all be staying on the ship, no colony."

"No, Five has desired this all along and the SUVI all agreed with her reasoning. The only real question was if she'd allow the former colonists to stay."

"And you didn't tell me?"

"I was waiting for you to pry it out of me, you know, with that way you have of getting information from me."

"Oh, I see. So, are you hiding any other secrets I should know about?"

"No, nothing at all."

"Really," grinned Linsey as she turned to pull her lover closer. "We'll just see about that."

While Linsey was interrogating Eighteen, Amanda cuddled Suvi-jean closer and held her while she brooded. "Penny for your thoughts."

"Huh? Oh, sorry sweetheart, I was just reviewing the adventures with this planet, and wondering what dangers we'll face at the next one. I just hope we all survive to get there."

"Jeannie?"

"I swear the next time an angry grounder starts demanding ..."

"Easy, sweetheart, easy. After your performance today, I doubt there'll be any of them in a hurry to demand anything from you any time soon."

"So you think it worked?"

"I do, yes. I think you've managed to settle that issue once and for all."

"Oh gods, I hope so. Mandy?"

"Yes?"

"I'm fussing. Can you do that thing you do to take my mind off my troubles?"

Amanda purred with delight. "With extreme pleasure, my darling SUVI, with extreme pleasure.

Three days later Suvi-jean and Amanda walked onto the bridge to find the First Officer there as well. "Captain on the bridge."

"As you were, people. First Officer, is the ship ready to sail?"

"Ship is locked down and ready to sail, Captain."

"Second Officer, is the bridge ready?"

"Course laid in and star drive on line, Captain."

Jeannie turned to the Earalithian at the pilot's station. "Pilot, are you ready?"

"Ready, Captain," he replied with a wide grin.

"Hit it."

He threw the switch and the mighty Reacher vanished from her orbit near a lonely star and hurtled through space at unimaginable speeds, on her way to the next star system and whatever wonders it might have to offer.

As the Reacher leaped out into space, Miriam Holbrooke sat with a group of former colonists. "So, no colony?"

"Not for us, no, but for our descendants, yes. Oh, I'm sure if we stumble across the perfect planet, Captain Sorenson will be more than happy to establish a colony, but until we do the idea is to gather resources and nurture a growing population. The long-term goal is still the same, people; the survival of the human race."

"Actually," sighed one man, "I confess I'm relieved. We're safe here on the ship and I'm too damned old for farming. Now that we know where we stand, and what the goals are, it will be a lot easier to find a way to fit ourselves in."

The discussion went on with a growing sense of relief. In truth, Elysium had broken the colony. It would be up to future generations for form the next one. For now, humans would be nomads, drifting through and exploring the wonders of the galaxy.

The End

Now folks, here's a quick peek at the next Forgotten World.

Survivor

by

Prudence MacLeod

Chapter 1

Shipwrecked

Jake White stifled a groan as he fought the blood from his eyes, desperate to regain his vision. Nearby he could hear the great beast that had dragged him here, snarling its defiance at the raging storm outside, the storm that had brought down their ship.

As he lay still trying to clear his senses something was poking painfully into his side. It was the big blaster, but the sharp edge pressing into his ribs told him the recoil pad had been lost. He dare not fire it without the pad, it would rip his shoulder off. Alas, he wasn't about to get a choice.

As Jake shifted his weight slightly a groan of pain was forced past his lips. With lightning speed, the beast turned and leaped at him. Rolling onto his back, he braced the damaged blaster against the stone floor and fired. Those deadly jaws were scant inches away when the point-blank blast hit the creature, hurling it out through the cave mouth and into the night.

With a groan Jake leaned his back against the cave wall. The ground had absorbed the blaster's recoil, saving his punctured shoulder further harm. Shaking off the encroaching darkness, he began to take inventory of his injuries. The beast had hit him from behind and carried him off, leaving a lot of bruises and a couple of puncture wounds. He'd need medical attention, but he could function.

"This a fine mess for a spoiled starship security guy to find himself in. Goddam primitive worlds anyway." He continued to mutter against his fate as he cut the sleeve from his tunic and used it to bandage the puncture wound on his upper arm. He was inspecting the wound on his thigh when he heard the low growl from the cave mouth.

"Well crap!" Jake groaned as he twisted around to brace the blaster for another shot. This wasn't the same animal, but there had been dozens of them. It didn't matter which one it was. As the snarling grew louder the four glowing eyes told him he had two visitors. Aiming the blaster as best he could, he pulled the trigger. Both animals were hurled away, but the mouth of the cave partially collapsed.

The next flash of lightning gave him a clear picture of how precarious the situation was. If he fired the blaster again it would bring the entire hillside down on him. Just as that realization sunk in, he heard the rocks at the cave mouth being pulled aside.

Another groan escaped his lips as he groped for and found the projectile weapon on his belt. The blaster fell aside as his other hand grasped the flashlight. Steadying his hand as best he could, Jake flicked on the light and took aim at the crumbled entrance.

"Don't shoot, it's only me." A grinning woman's face appeared in the light, then she wriggled inside and came to him. "Hey Jake, how's it going?"

"It's been better. Twenty, how did you find me?"

"I could find you anywhere, Handsome."

"Stop it, woman, you'll get me killed."

"Jake?"

"You've been flirting with me for weeks, and as much as I enjoy it, I'm married, you're married, and ..."

"I'm SUVI?" She was a SUVI, survivor of unknown viral infection, one of twenty survivors out of nine thousand plus humans infected. SUVI, no longer human, but part human and part something else.

"Yes, you're SUVI, but that's a plus, not a minus. Twenty, I'll admit you scare the hell out of me."

"Oh?" She continued to poke and prod gently at his injuries, adjusting his bandaging job, plus adding a few of her own from the pack at her side. "I grabbed a first aid kit as I left the ship. There you go, all patched up. So, tell me why I scare you."

"I can't read you. Jeannie has taught me pretty well, and I can read most of the SUVI, but not you, you're different."

She settled down beside him, took the pistol from his hand and fired at the opening. There was a yowl of pain outside then silence. "And that's bad because?"

He sighed then groaned as he tried to shift to look into her eyes. "It's bad because I can't read you, I can't tell if you're playing or not. If you are, then all well and good, every guy's ego swells when a gorgeous woman flirts with him, and I'm no different."

"So you think I'm attractive?"

"Stop it, woman. You know damn well I do. If you're not just playing, then I'm well and truly screwed."

"I don't understand. What are you saying here?"

"Twenty, I'm saying if you're serious here I doubt I'll be able to resist you, but it'll destroy me utterly. I'll lose Carla, I'll lose the respect of the captain, my friends, all the credibility I've carefully built up with my fellow officers as well as the crew and passengers. Right now I'm utterly tormented."

To his great surprise she sidled closer and laid her head on his shoulder. "I hadn't thought about any of that, Jake, and I'm sorry for it. Let me tell you a story now. Half of me once had a husband and a good marriage, but that actually ended over thirty years ago, I personally never have, and I don't now. Eamon and I decided that too much has changed, and he released me."

"Okay."

"Now, about you and me. You know I'm super intuitive, even more so than Eighteen. Since I first met you I've known there was something special about you, that you hold something important for me. I guess I started flirting with you to get your attention."

"It worked."

Her sweet rich laughter echoed through the cavern, bringing a sloppy grin to his face. "All right, Jake, I've been set free, but you haven't. So, a little light flirting is all you get."

"Promise?"

"Well not forever, you're not that handsome."

This time it was his laughter that rang through the cavern, but his cracked ribs changed the laugh into a racking cough. "Oh gods, Jake, I'm sorry."

"Sure you are."

"I am, silly human. Jake, you're a vital part of the Reacher's success and survival. The captain depends on you, and I owe her much. The crew and passengers look to you to keep order. No, no, don't try to deny it. We have something important for each other, you and I, but we'll keep it light and friendly."

He could see the desire as well as the determination in her eyes now and knew that, although she didn't want it this way, she would make it happen and he sighed with relief. "For the greater good?"

"Yes, Jake, for the greater good. So, you do understand SUVI."

"I'm getting there. Now, back to the situation at hand. Put that magic SUVI brain to work and figure out how we're going to get out of here and back to the ship."

"Not to worry, it's getting light out."

"And that's good because?"

"These creatures are nocturnal. With any luck there won't be a lot of daylighters to contend with."

"What about the storm?"

"It won't let up for a day or two. Hungry?"

"Yeah, I am." He watched in amazement as she pulled a couple of ration bars from the pack at her side. "So, you stopped to pack a picnic before you came looking for me?"

She chuckled at that. "Actually, I packed this bag before we left the Reacher. Something just told me the Explorer would run into trouble. You were hell bent on going along because things on the Reacher were boring lately."

"That's why you insisted on coming along? Because I did?"

"Because I knew you'd get into trouble, I knew you'd be hurt, but I didn't know the outcome. Yes, I came for you. Happy now?"

"Now I'm really scared." Again, her laughter brought a smile to his face.

Also by Prudence MacLeod

Forgotten Worlds
Suvi
Echo of the Past
Survivors

Watch for more at https://www.prudencemacleod.com/.

About the Author

Jennifer Crandall writes and publishes under three different names, Prudence MacLeod, J.L.Crandall, and Jenni Leigh. Learn more about her on her website,

Read more at https://www.prudencemacleod.com/.

www.ingramcontent.com/pod-product-compliance
Lightning Source LLC
Chambersburg PA
CBHW020947180626
46814CB00003B/966